Winterwood

A Novel

PATRICK McCABE

BLOOMSBURY

Published by Bloomsbury USA, New York
Distributed to the trade by Macmillan

All papers used by Bloomsbury USA are natural, recyclable
products made from wood grown in well-managed
forests. The manufacturing processes conform to the
environmental regulations of the country of origin.

THE LIBRARY OF CONGRESS HAS CATALOGED THE HARDCOVER EDITION AS FOLLOWS:

McCabe, Patrick, 1955–
Winterwood : a novel / Patrick McCabe.—1st U.S. ed.
p. cm.
ISBN-13: 978-1-59691-163-5 (hardcover)
ISBN-10: 1-59691-163-8 (hardcover)
1. Social change—Ireland—Fiction. 2. Mountain life—Ireland—Fiction.
3. Life change events—Fiction. 4. Storytellers—Fiction. 5. Ireland—Fiction.
6. Psychological fiction.
I. Title.

PR6063.C32W56 2006
823'.914—dc22
2006015837

Originally published in the United Kingdom by Bloomsbury in 2006
First published in the United States by Bloomsbury USA in 2007
This paperback edition published in 2008

Paperback ISBN-10: 1-59691-513-7
ISBN-13: 978-1-59691-513-8

1 3 5 7 9 10 8 6 4 2

Typeset by Hewer Text UK Ltd, Edinburgh
Printed in the United States of America by Quebecor World Fairfield

To Katie McCabe

Eighties

One: My Journey Westward,
My Old Mountain Home

IT WAS THE AUTUMN of 1981 and I'd been asked by my paper the *Leinster News* to do an article on folklore and changing ways in Ireland, a chance I jumped at, availing myself of the opportunity to return home to Slievenageeha, which I hadn't been to visit in years.

And was more than glad that I did, as it happened, for quite unexpectedly it turned out to be festival week, with a ceilidh starting up as I drove into town. On a crude platform in the square a slap-bass combo was banging away goodo, with a whiskery old-timer sawing at his fiddle, stomping out hornpipes to beat the band. He must have been close on seventy years of age, with a curly copper thatch and this great unruly rusty beard touched through-out with streaks of silver. He slapped his thighs and whooped and catcalled, encouraging anyone who knew it to join in the 'traditional come-all-you'!

Who, by the looks of things, weren't exactly a multitude – in fact, nobody at all seemed to know the words.

Presumably because prosperity had begun to take hold of the valley with such ballads being perceived now as somewhat out of date. There was no shortage, however, of spirited shouts of approval:

—Good man, Ned! You never lost it!

—He's a good one, Auld Pappie, make no mistake!

As the band cheered and chorded along merrily, the lyrics sailing out over the tall pine trees:

Well don't we look sweet as here we both lie
My partner for ever just him and I
Like lovers betrothed in the cold stony clay
From peep of the sun until the end of the day.

In keeping with the 'good old days' theme, everyone had dressed up in britches and brogues, with not a modern conveyance in sight, nothing but a motley assortment of charabancs and carts. There were livestock shows and cattle auctions, horse-pulling contests and a poultry competition. A woman in a bonnet offered to sell me 'the choicest' free-range eggs. I thanked her profusely but politely declined, regretting it somewhat, I have to say, when she mentioned my father. She told me she'd known him well.

—Ah yes! she said. Auld Daddy Hatch – sure we all knew each other, back in those days!

I met the old fiddler by chance later on. His face was livid-red now and I watched him as he flung the instrument on the table with undisguised disdain. He told me he'd been drinking all day. I asked him would he consider being

4

interviewed for the paper? He said yes – on one condition. I would have to play host with a 'clatter of drinks'.

I readily agreed as he regarded me intently through narrow, suspicious eyes. When I was ordering, the barman shook my hand and heartily welcomed me to Slievenageeha. I told him I'd been born here and was overjoyed to be back.

—It's always nice to welcome our own, he said cheerily, before adding: And I see you've already met Auld Pappie – the wild and woolly rascal from the hills!

—I have indeed, I said, and what a fine musician he is! He handed me the drinks and laughed.

—Oh, he's a musician all right – but then, of course, he'd be a fiddler by nature! Ha ha!

When I asked him what he meant he tossed back his head and told me he was only joking. Adding with a conspiratorial wink as I turned to go:

—Just be careful of them auld stories of his. You wouldn't know whether to believe them or not. He's an awful man once he gets going. Tells everyone he spent years in America. And sure the poor auld fucker – he's never once left the valley. Never set foot outside Slievenageeha. Now, there's your drinks, welcome home and thanks very much!

As soon as I came back to join my companion with the drinks, I could tell that he had been listening to every word we'd said.

—Don't mind that barman, he snorted as I sat down, sure the poor auld fool is fucking doting. He's not from the mountain at all, in fact. He's not one of us. Fuck him and ride his wife, Redmond. Ha ha. Cheers! *Slainte mhaith, a mhic og an chnoic! Failte abhaile.*

5

To your good health, young son of the mountain. Welcome home.

We remained in the pub until well after closing time and then he invited me up to his house — if that's what you'd call it. It took us nearly half an hour to get there, winding our way up a rugged hilly track, pushing our way through a plantation of firs, through tangled copsewood and green depths of fern. Eventually arriving at a tumbledown shack, evidently constructed from any materials that happened to be at hand. Random tufts of grass sprouted wildly from its roof.

When we got inside, he lit a candle and pressed it down into the middle of the table. A silhouette began forming ever so slowly on the wall. He chucked the cork from the whiskey with his teeth, throwing me this odd look as he spat it away, locating, at length, two filthy mugs.

—So you're Daddy Hatch's son. Well, isn't that a good one! he said, lighting up a 'stogie', planking himself down in the creaking rocking chair.

—He was a great man for the cards, your father. Him and Florian, that brother of his. Like a lot of men from about the valley, it was hard to tell the pair of them apart. It be's hard for strangers trying to do that — tell us menfolk one from the other, with our great big beards and red curly heads. Some says that we does it on purpose, take refuge behind our close-knit tribe so nobody can ever get blamed — for the wicked things we get up to sometimes. Like your father, for example, God bless us but he gave that poor mother of yours an awful life. Matter of fact, I seen him kicking her one night. Hitting her a kick right up the backside, and Florian there doing nothing, only laughing his head off, on account of she didn't bring him his drink quick enough. And then, be the hokey, what do you know but she goes and dies and her still a young woman! Not that he went kind of odd or anything like that. Oh no. We're made of much hardier stuff than that about here. Anyhow it meant he could devote all his time now entirely to the cards. Isn't that right, Mr Hatch?

He tapped his foot and looked at me, twinkling. I didn't answer him. I was much too taken aback by his forthrightness.

—You'll see a lot of changes, Redmond, he said, it ain't like the old place any more.

I coughed, with a ridiculously incongruous politeness. Partly, I have to admit, to disguise my inadequacy. I had been so long away, I was at a loss to make any kind of proper response.

—There certainly have been a lot of changes, I agreed, now that we're entering the modern world, I suppose.

He nodded as he continued rocking to and fro. Said nothing for some considerable time. Then he elevated his stocky bulk and said:

—I want to tell you something and I want you to remember this, Redmond, my friend.

He stared directly at me.

—The mountain doesn't go away. It doesn't go away – you hear?

He stiffened sharply, his brows knitting tensely.

—You *hear*? he repeated. I'm talking to you – what's wrong, are you *deaf*?

He flicked the stogie as he continued obsessively:

—Once upon a time, Redmond. There was this woman. The old woman. The old woman, what was she doing? She was sitting in her cabin. Sitting in her cabin late one night. A simple little homestead the very same as this, doing her knitting and sitting in the chair. Just rocking away like I'm doing now. Then all of a sudden she heard it. She heard the noise. At first she thought: It's nothing, I'll think no more about it. But then what happened, she heard it again. She heard it again, Redmond. Then looked up and saw it standing there. She saw its shadow first, you see, then slowly looked up and saw it standing before her. Standing right there before her – staring down. Looking at her with these two dead eyes. There was no feeling in them, Redmond. They were dead, them eyes. You know what they were like? Two black holes. Like two black holes bored right into its skull. It wasn't a human being, Redmond. It was a *creature*. A *thing* that had come creeping around there that night. Them was hard times, Redmond. That's how it was in these rural places – and you know it. Them memories, they don't just up and walk away. You reckon them memories just get up and walk?

I wasn't sure what to say. I just shook my head and stared blankly at the floor, swirling the colourless liquor in my mug.

—No, I replied.

—That's right, Redmond, he went on, they don't. They last as long as them fucking pine trees. Till there's frost in hell, Redmond. Did you hear me singing that verse today?

Before I could respond, his fiddle had appeared as if by

8

magic and the bow was sweeping up and down as he
scraped:

> How long will we lie here O Lord who can tell?
> Till the winter snow whitens the high hills of hell.
> Till the winter snow whitens the high hills of hell!

He flung the instrument away and spat disdainfully:

—That's right. That's how long. That's how long – and
don't you forget it! Don't you forget it, Redmond Hatch!

A crooked branch tapped softly against the window. The
tobacco smoke wafted desultorily in the silence, floating
past the black glass pane. We sat there surrounded by
swarming shadows, which seemed to lunge forward before
retreating once more, as if in the throes of some nether-
worldly game.

He said that he'd tell me anything I wanted to know. There
was nothing he didn't know about the valley, he said.

—Ned's the boy who knows his history, he insisted, for
he's been here longer than any of the bastards. Ever since
Old God's time, he laughed. I went to school with your
father and your Uncle Florian. Florian thought he was the
toughest customer going. He was in a knife fight once.
That's where he got the scar on his cheek. And do you know
who it was that gave it to him? Do you know who it was
who gave him that scar, Red?

He turned his finger into his chest.

—Muggins, he snorted, swelling with mirth.

He used many phrases familiar to me from my childhood.

9

—Fucking muggins, he laughed again, before rising from the chair and looming over me.

—I made this myself, he told me, liberally refilling our mugs with a flourish, genuine 'clear' from Slievenageeha Mountain. That's what me and your daddy used to call it. Your father, by cripes, I never seen a man hardier. He'd have supped that clear till it streamed out his ears. Here – help yourself to another drop there, Redmond! By the time we've got a good drunk on us there'll be more crack in this valley than the night I pissed on the electric fence!

I did as he said. And, boy, was Ned right. That old clear, it went slipping down a treat. As he observed whilst weaving his way back from the dresser:

—It tasted so nice that it tasted like more! It tasted like more, Redmond!

So much more, in fact, that I didn't manage to make it home at all. All I remember is standing there with him outside the cabin, as we gazed far down into the valley below where the skeletal girders of the new shopping mall were starkly outlined against the spreading night sky. He told me about the proposed motorway.

—They're even talking about a casino, he said, The Gold Club they're gonna call it. I'm thinking they're getting above their raising, my friend. Anyhow, it'll never happen.

—*Haw*! he grunted, *Haw*! and slapped me resoundingly across the back.

I staggered blearily, but contentedly, back down the winding track, calling Catherine from the phone box in the town and stammering out some laughable excuse. I realised afterwards, of course, that I needn't have bothered my head being worried. There was absolutely no need to be making up excuses. Not in those days. For Catherine and me, we had been getting on like a house on fire. You could tell by the sound of her voice that she wasn't perturbed in the least. Just so long as I was enjoying myself, she said. That was all she cared about.

—I'm glad you went, I heard her say, I've always felt it's something you needed to do, go back to Slievenageeha, your old mountain home.

—Thanks, sugar lips, I said, blowing a kiss down the phone.

'Sugar lips' was one of our private and intimate exchanges. I know it sounds corny but we kind of loved it.

When I got back to the house, Ned was standing with his fiddle at the ready.

—'The Pride of Erin'! he cried out and began vigorously fingering a soaring jig, bellowing with gusto: 'Round the flure and shift the dresser!'

—More clear? I asked him, grinning like a half-idiot, with a down-home casualness, entirely unconvincing.

I was still pretty unsteady as I stood beside him with the bottle.

—May the giving hand never falter – a gentleman and a scholar is what you are, Redmond! A son of your father's – a bucking son of your father's!

When I looked again the moon had disappeared, faded into a shining silver sun.

*　　*　　*

11

After that, I began to visit the valley regularly. I'd be so eager to get out of the city on Fridays, looking forward to more of Ned's stories about life in the valley and the days of long ago. There seemed to be no end to his tales, each one wilder than the next. There were stories about card playing, drink-binging and women, cattle raids and horse racing and ceilidhs that had gone on for weeks. You definitely, at times, did get the impression that he was making them up as he went along.

I always seemed to arrive when he was in the middle of feeding his chickens. He had ten or eleven Buff Orpingtons he kept in a coop. There was nothing the kids from the new estates liked better than to be allowed up there, to have a yarn with good old 'Pappie', and keep him company as he fed his fowl. Especially little Michael Gallagher, the happy-go-lucky fellow with the freckles who was forever singing.

—I'm the bestest friend of Ned, he used to say to me.

The mothers and fathers were crazy about Ned. They were 'cracked about him', you'd hear them saying. Especially the mothers. They said he was 'a tonic', and 'terrific with the kids'. Absolutely great to have around the place.

The most recent development was his teaching of the fiddle. Everyone I spoke to was over the moon about that too. I interviewed a few of the mothers and they told me that as far as they were concerned having characters like Ned in the community was a great way for their children to find out about an Ireland that was fast disappearing – if not, indeed, practically vanished already.

You'd see him strolling about the place laughing, nodding to the parents as he whistled some jig. Or chatting away with them, spinning them some yarn, as they left their kids in for 'Ned's children's ceilidh'. He ran that now in the schoolhouse at weekends. He'd have known most of the old families, of course. Could roll off their names at the drop of a hat. They absolutely loved the way he talked, all these phrases you only heard in old-time speech. Half-forgotten proverbs only dimly remembered. All Ned had to do was say something like:

—I met Auld Quirke on his way up the road and he'd a face on him, ladies, like an ass eating thistles!

And, without exception, he'd have them laughing like lunatics, wetting themselves, practically. They just couldn't get enough of Ned Strange's conversation.

—You can't beat Auld Pappie, you'd hear them say, a card and no mistake. What would Slievenageeha be like without him? A very, very dull place indeed, whatever progress we might make in the future.

They'd always wave as they went driving past.

—There he is – our own Auld Pappie!

As Ned looked up from his chickens and smiled. It really was an appropriate name: Auld Pappie.

As Ned fed his chickens and whistled his jigs, the perfect picture of contented old age.

In a way I suppose it was as if he himself were some kind of noble, immovable, magisterial mountain, which seemed to have existed, literally, for centuries. Long before progress of any kind began.

—Since the very first of the angels got chased, as he

might have put it himself, since the very first angel was fucked out of heaven!

Now and then it would occur to me that something he'd said – or the manner in which he'd said it – somehow just didn't seem to fit. That he'd been trying too *hard* to impress me or something. Sometimes he'd even mimic my accent to my face. Other times there'd be this look – I didn't like it. It made me feel queasy, ill-at-ease.

There was one particular evening – I find it humiliating to recall. He rested his chin on his hand and pulled his chair up next to mine. Then grinned.

—Your father and me went to the ceilidh in Athleague. Your Uncle Florian was there. Boys, we drank more porter that evening so we did. And then we started into the hornpipes. Florian took his britches down and began to dance in the middle of the hall. Boys, me and your auld fellow we had ourselves a laugh! Because Florian, as you know, was a divil for the dancing. There wasn't a hornpipe in the book but he knew. And your father too, he had his moments. Oh, yes, me auld son, Daddy Hatch and his brother Florian were well known in this valley. You should be proud of them, they were a credit to the mountain, your beloved caring family. Even if they did put you into the orphanage – ha ha!

He didn't flinch for a second. I could feel my cheeks burning. He just sat there twinkling, saying nothing at all. I was on the verge of protesting when, out of the blue, he lifted his leg, his shoulders heaving as he blithely expelled wind.

14

—A reg'lar arse-cracker – the best today!

Before I could say anything he had opened another bottle of clear.

When I looked up again the sun's pale fire was lighting up the sky.

In the aftermath of our 'session', I attributed my reticence to my predictable, pedantic, assumed new suburbanism. I'd simply been away too long, I reasoned, and had become more or less disconnected, alienated from the life I'd once known, as it once had been lived on the bare and barren mountain, in a sleepy little town which didn't even feature on the map. I had lost the skills. I hadn't it in me. I was much too conscious of embarrassment and unpleasantness. And he knew it. He knew I'd do almost anything to avoid confrontation. Which suited his purposes admirably, indeed perfectly. There was nothing he liked more than playing games.

To put it plainly, he was amusing himself. Toying with me, really – what else could you call it?

I consoled myself by thinking that if I had become debilitatingly civilised and grown apart from my people and background, then at least I wasn't alone, for everyone in the valley was doing exactly that – if the gaudy identikit housing was anything to go by, not to mention the transatlantic accents and the sprawling housing developments, with names more appropriate to Surrey than Slievenageeha: 'Meadow Vale', 'Primrose Demesne', 'The Chantries'.

Which was why Ned, unencumbered as he was by any new and imported orthodoxy, had, by common consent, come to embody the authentic spirit of heritage and tradition. It was as if it had been decided that simply having Ned was sufficient. That was enough to keep them in touch with their fast-fading traditions and customs of the past.

—*Chuck chuck*! you'd hear them laughing, as yet another 'Ned story' was uproariously related.

—My mother used to keep chickens too, you know, in our own backyard, way back when times were simpler.

—Isn't it great all the same, to have someone like Ned? Otherwise our kids would never know anything about our history.

—Sometimes I think we're losing our soul, do you know that Mrs?

—Not while Ned is here to remind us. He'll make sure we don't lose our way.

—Now you're talking. 'The Pride of Erin' and 'Jenny's Chickens'.

'Jenny's Chickens' – that was another favourite reel of his.

—*Chuck chuck*! they'd laugh.

—*Chuck chuck chuck*!

—*Chuck chuck chuck*, thank God for Ned Strange!

It was the very first time I'd witnessed his anger and seen the depths of which he was capable. I was in no hurry to see it again. Even now I shudder, thinking of it. He had happened to come upon the old book by accident. It was an ancient and decrepit volume, sickeningly musty. His voice was trembling as he turned its sodden pages. I could just about make out the title beneath his thumb, lettered in flaking gold leaf. *The Heart's Enchantment*, it read.

—*Look*! he spat, his fucking name is on it. 'John Olson'. He gave it to her as a present, the miserable fucking whore. I knew I wasn't wrong. I wasn't wrong about Annamarie Gordon!

It was the first time he'd ever mentioned Olson in my company. John Olson was a local man who'd made his fortune in the US.

—He thought he owned the place, he went on, used to drive around in this big fancy limousine Cadillac. You shoulda seen that conceited face. I've decided to honour you with my presence. So you can count yourselves lucky. You can count yourselves lucky, mongrel scum. That's what Olson was thinking to himself. That's what that look of his was saying, Redmond. *Look at me* – so what do you think? Am I king of the mountain or am I not? Are you lucky or not to have me home? O Slievenageeha, I think that you are. I think that you are very fortunate indeed. And I should know. After all, I'm Mr John. I'm Mr *John fucking Olson*!

He scrunched the stogie beneath the heel of his boot.

—Cunt, he said. Cunt and hoor: I'd as lief have cut his throat. As true as I'm standing here in my own fucking kitchen. Do you hear me, Redmond? Are you listening to me, boy?

I kept hoping against hope that his mood would change – as it so often did, without any warning. That he'd, out of

17

nowhere, erupt into laughter, insisting then that it had all been a joke.

He didn't, however. He just stood there in silence, picking at the damp book as it disintegrated in his hands. Staring, with a fierce and deeply troubling tenacity of purpose, at the blurred italicised signature: 'To Annamarie from John Olson with love, Slievenageeha 1963'.

I began to dread hearing John Olson's name. But whether I did or whether I didn't didn't seem to amount to a whole lot of consequence.

—I'm not sorry for what I done to him, he'd bawl. That was why I went to America, Redmond. They think I didn't go. They think I never went near the States. That's what they say. That's what they'll tell you down in the pub. That's what he told you that first night. I know. I heard him. Auld Ned would never be able to do the like of that. He'd never ever stray beyond these hills. These hills are his home, the only home he knows.

He hissed:

—But that's where they're wrong. For Ned did stray. He *did* go to America. He went there – and a lot of other places too. But they'll never know, the ignorant fools.

I tried to come up with an excuse to get out. But it was as if he was defying me to do exactly that. He persisted with his monologue. I had never heard anything quite so venomous, even from his mouth. I shifted uneasily in the chair. He looked at me accusingly.

—You want to say something. To me. What is it you want to say, Redmond?

—You said you did something – to John Olson, I said. What was it you did, Ned?

—I hurt him bad. I cut him with a blade. No I didn't. I beat him. I beat him to within an inch of his life. That's what I did to Olson the snake, Redmond.

His eyes filled up with loathing. I caught a glimpse of my ashen face in the window.

—Why did you have to do that? I asked him.

It sounded stupid. I can see that now. I ought to have said nothing.

He teased his beard and then, all of a sudden, snapped:

—*Why?* Did I hear you say *why*, Redmond? Because he deserved it, you stupid cunt! He deserved it on account of him and my Annamarie!

It was as if all the shadows in the room had suddenly decided to converge on my chair. As though, collectively, to pose that very same conundrum: why are you asking stupid questions, Redmond?

Foolishly, I had spilt some of the clear down my jacket. You could see that he had noticed, but had decided to let it pass. He upended his mug and broodily continued:

—Some people say that if a woman does you wrong, that if she happens to stray from the conjugal bower, then what you got to do, what your responsibility is, is to search in your heart and see if you can extend her some small measure of forgiveness. But me, I don't happen to believe that, you see, Redmond. I searched in my heart all right but I couldn't find anything that was of any use to me in there. Nothing. I tried Jesus too – him and all his other do-good

19

cronies. But they were no use neither. Nope. No good, my boy. Not worth a flying fuck. Do you find that disappointing, Redmond? Well if you do, I apologise for that. Anyway, it had upset me so bad I had to ask her again. Annamarie my darling, I said to her, why did you do it? Why did you let Olson put it in you, his tallywhacker? But she wouldn't tell me – just kept on saying she *hadn't* permitted it. Until I swear, my friend Redmond, I swear I couldn't take it any more and says to her: Annamarie you know now what's gonna happen. No, she says, what is it? Annamarie, I says, it's the cellar. Oh no, she says, not the cellar. Yes I'm afraid it is, I said. But, you know – you know the saddest thing, Redmond? She never repented. Not once. Every time I looked in her eyes I could see she was still thinking of him. That old snake – he was still on her mind. Damn near broke my heart so it did.

—So what did you do? I asked him. My saliva formed a thick and distasteful ball inside my mouth.

He lowered his eyes and gazed at the floor. Then he raised them again and flashed his incisors. The look he gave me chilled my blood.

—You'd like to know, wouldn't you? Who knows – maybe I'll tell you. Maybe I'll tell you one day, just how it ended between us. Between me and the lovely Annamarie Gordon.

It was the last thing I wanted to hear, anything connected with good loving gone bad. For in those days my marriage to Catherine was close to perfect. A flawless union. The sort of partnership people dream about. We'd met at a dance in

July 1980, in a town in County Cork where I'd been covering some local story. I can't even remember what it was now. She was one of the Courtneys, a well-known merchant family in the area. Her beauty was unique: it's as simple as that. It was unusual to find someone like her working in a bar, I remember suggesting to her. She laughed and said she'd been studying at UCC, history and philosophy, but had failed her finals and not bothered repeating.

—These things happen, I said, somewhat vacantly, discreetly trying to avoid her lovely green-blue eyes.

We ended up dating and within three or four weeks – well, if you're talking about enchantment of the heart then all I can say is I came to know quite a bit about that particular subject. Not to put too fine a point on it, I fell head over heels in love with Catherine Courtney. Telling her things I'd never have told anyone.

Which was regrettable, obviously, in the light of what happened.

I made it my business to travel down from Dublin whenever I could. I used to love sitting in the pub with her while she had her lunch. She told me she adored the musician John Martyn – at that time I'd never even heard of him. A situation which I went about rectifying straight away and the next time we met, I presented her with an album of his called *Grace & Danger*. There was a track on it she grew to love. It was called 'Sweet Little Mystery' and any time I heard it, it thrilled me. It was as if John Martyn had somehow known. If that doesn't sound too foolish. A lot of what she said I never even heard – too busy staring at her lips or at her hair. Then one day I found myself saying:

—Catherine Courtney, will you marry me?

I hadn't given her any warning at all.

—Yes, she said. Yes, Redmond, I will, leaning forward and taking my hand.

I couldn't believe my luck. I just sat there staring in silence – like a simpleton. Then she laughed and kissed me on the cheek. She was wearing a silver necklace which she fingered a little nervously, abstractedly playing with the dangling charm, a shining initial, the letter 'C'.

—Look at you! she said and laughed again, a tincture of pink appearing on her cheek.

We were married exactly six months after that, in 1981. I was forty and she was twenty-two but the age difference didn't matter one whit. That was what she had said and that was what I knew.

It was the greatest day of my life. No question.

We rented a basement flat in Dublin, in the south city suburb of leafy Rathmines, in an old rambling rundown Georgian house in Cowper Road. It wasn't much but it was all we could afford. It didn't matter, we told ourselves – it wouldn't always be like this. Sooner or later our ship would come in.

—And who knows, maybe we'll be able to afford a mansion, she used to say, tossing her scarf back, with a kind of impish devil-may-care laugh.

At weekends we used to visit houses that were for sale –

just for amusement and something to do. There was one she took a special shine to. It was situated in the suburb of Rathfarnham, on Ballyroan Road. It had a lovely little apple orchard out the back. I could tell by her expression that she really loved that house.

—Maybe one day, love, I remember saying, squeezing her arm as we strode towards the bus stop.

You'd hear her humming and it would do your heart good. She was humming it on the bus that day going home.

It's just that sweet little mystery that's here in your heart
It's just that sweet little mystery makes me cry.

I continued working for the *Leinster News*, serialising my articles and going down to visit Ned. Rathmines then was a lovely place to live and Catherine got work in the various bars, frequented in the main by students. I used to meet her in the Sunset Grill after work, a little place not far from the library. Our treats at that time were Knickerbocker Glories.

It was stupid, I know. Love makes you like that.

We continued living in Cowper Road. Then our firstborn, a girl, arrived two years later, in March 1983. We decided to call her Imogen, after Catherine's grandmother. She was a wonder, really. To look at, to listen to, everything. Every day I woke up she filled my heart with pride. Catherine Courtney had been given to me as a gift. And now there was Imogen. She had her mother's looks – the green-blue eyes and the very same laugh. I used to take her in the evenings and wheel her buggy through the streets of Rathmines, before we'd meet her mother in the Sunset Grill, after her shift had ended in the pub.

You looked at Imogen's curls and felt guilty – why, you thought, should you be so privileged? Occasionally I'd receive a bonus and I'd arrive home unexpectedly with a present – an album or a book for Catherine, maybe, and something from the Early Learning Centre for Immy. That was what I called her now. The odd time we'd get down to Slattery's for a pint – if the girl upstairs offered to babysit. But generally we didn't bother. We didn't want to, to tell the honest truth. We were just as happy to sit and listen to John Martyn or watch *Dallas* on the telly. *Dallas* – we were crazy about that.

—I lawrv you *Jay-Aw*! Catherine used to say.

It became a kind of catchphrase of ours.

—I lawrv you *Jay-Aw*! we'd laugh, as Immy gurgled and Catherine sat in the firelight, reading, wiggling her toes as she serenely turned the pages.

On my way into work, I would find myself lapsing into a daydream, unable to understand what it was I had done to deserve such bounteous, unmitigated good fortune. But then nothing, of course, nothing, is ever as simple as that.

You should never really expect it to be.

We had been in Rathmines for almost four years and fully intended to carry on doing just that when, in March 1985, the *Leinster News* unexpectedly went into liquidation and, after months of looking around the city with little or no success, I was on the verge of becoming really worried when

– quite out of the blue – I was offered a position with a small newspaper in London: the *North London Chronicle*. Which, at first – I won't pretend otherwise – I was quite hesitant about. It seemed such a big step with a young child and everything. And details of the salary were vague, to say the least. But after some time talking it over, Catherine suggested that I ought to take it. She had been toying with the idea of going back to college, she said, for some time. And London would provide lots of opportunities – perhaps it was time for us to broaden our horizons.

To make a long story short, I called them and accepted.

We moved to London some weeks later and initially things, I have to say, they looked really positive. But then, unfortunately, fate intervened and we encountered, I suppose, what you might call another small piece of misfortune. The *North London Chronicle* was bought out by a rival and the core staff – including me – were let go without a settlement. Initially, there was a lot of bellicose talk in the pub, with the union official pledging retribution and vengeance. But in the end, as I had anticipated, his passionate belligerence all came to nothing.

But even then, Catherine Courtney and I remained undaunted, picking up pieces of work here and there. I spent a while on a freesheet in Cricklewood and Catherine did stretches in an off-licence called Victoria Wine and various cafés and bars. Then we discovered that if one of us didn't work we would actually be better off, qualifying both for income support and housing benefit. We debated it for a while but then I decided that I could work from home, submitting articles on a freelance basis. It worked like a dream – dropping Immy to the nursery every day, before coming home to sit down at my typewriter. With the result being that, against all the odds, we found ourselves now attaining an altogether new level of happiness. Something neither of us would have ever considered possible. Considering how contented we had been to begin with. It really was quite remarkable. And it made me feel so – why, just so proud. All I kept thinking was: the miraculous things that, in adversity, can happen to an ordinary man and woman. Just so long as they're fortunate enough to be in love. There is no happiness or joy that can come close to the feelings you experience in such a blessed situation. I picked up Imogen every day at the same time, chatting to her the whole way home. Such a chatterbox she was becoming!

We always had great fun walking through Queen's Park, with her sucking her lollipop and me singing the theme tune from *My Little Pony*, shouting 'Kimono!' and 'Pinky Pie!', the names of all the characters she loved. Sometimes we'd just stop and sit there in the park, telling stories – but that often wasn't such a good idea. For no sooner would you have finished than she'd want you to start all over again. Of course it would irritate you sometimes, if you'd been having articles rejected or whatever. But nonetheless you always did. Once we were in the little café and she started sobbing.

—What's wrong, pet? I asked her, alarmed.

She pointed to the ground where a great stag beetle was lying on its back, as a column of ants made off with its innards.

—Don't let the mini-beasts get me, Daddy! she wept.

—I won't! I assured her and took her in my arms.

She was still sobbing a little bit.

—Miss Greene says the mini-beasts are our friends. But if they were, they wouldn't do that!

—Mummy! she would squeal when Catherine was with us. Daddy tells stories – about the Snowman!

She couldn't get enough of that Raymond Briggs story. She watched the video over and over. She'd just sit there, rapt, with her tense shoulders up, as off he went, the little snowman waltzing, right out across the rooftops of the world.

The new Kilburn flat we got off the housing association – it really looked fantastic now. The things that woman Catherine could do with interiors – she had completely and utterly transformed the place. And Imogen, by all accounts, was the playgroup star. They were always telling me what a character she was. They really were such beautiful times. All the more reason I was completely unprepared for it when I came home one day after buying a present, a polly pocket for Imogen's birthday, and discovered Catherine in our bedroom with a man.

Once, having been mugged outside a pub in Hackney, I had realised, to my astonishment, that in such situations the anger you expect is not what you feel. In its place this banal and bewildering *numbness*. That was what I felt as I stood there, turning the polly pocket around in my hand.

I had no idea who he was. I had never laid eyes on him before. I remember thinking he looked Greek or perhaps Turkish. In fact he was Maltese.

We had these pink roses Catherine had planted in the garden: twining away there, so delicate and fragile. All I could see were those baby-pink roses, spreading right out across the neatly tonsured grass.

I continued to write my articles, regularly submitting them to various magazines. But I didn't, unfortunately, have very much success. Which isn't all that surprising. They were hopelessly digressive and quite badly written, in retrospect. I just couldn't seem to keep my mind on the subject. Sometimes the pen would literally fall from my hand. Once, sitting at my typewriter, I could have sworn I saw Imogen, naked and blue, shivering with the cold, trying to catch my attention outside the window. It seemed so real I almost cried out. Before realising, at the last moment, that she was safe and asleep upstairs in bed, with her favourite duvet tucked up to her chin – the one with Zippy and Bungle, her friends out of *Rainbow*. It was stress that was making me think like that. I knew it was. That was what I told myself. You could hardly expect to experience marital difficulties without there being some outward manifestation of your inner anxieties, I reasoned.

I decided to work harder at keeping us together. We'd been through too much to let it slip now. That was my state of mind, essentially, at the time. That was how I viewed our situation.

Then one day I came home and the house was deserted.

There was a note on the mantelpiece saying Catherine's solicitor would be in touch. You should never lift your hand to your wife. It's wrong, pure and simple. It's like something a throwback from the mountain might do, and nothing can excuse it in any circumstances.

The hearing took place in early 1989, and after that, they returned to Dublin for good. Now on my own, London began to seem quite threatening and disorientating. It seemed, quite wilfully, to slide back its once-genial mask, coldly disavowing its formerly benign past. I was taken aback. I hadn't been expecting that. And it distressed me deeply – I won't deny it.

I'd wake in the night, in the iron grip of unease. Having sensed this chilling *presence* in the room.

I could feel it standing stock-still beside me. It was a horrible time.

But spending my days drinking wasn't going to help things. I knew that. But nonetheless it didn't stop me doing it. I'd promise myself I would reform my ways. I'd wake up and say: 'Today I'm going to make the effort.' Then, almost immediately after this welcome and invigorating surge of new strength, I'd find myself helplessly thinking: They're gone.

And, before I knew it, would be sitting, as before, in some anonymous poorly lit pub. Some half-forgotten Irish labourers' bar where the curtains hadn't been washed in years, where Enya music played on a loop and old men wilted in corners, doing their best to anaesthetise themselves. I think I gravitated towards those pubs because just by sitting in them I could construct a pretty accurate picture of my future. A facsimile of the past the old men were defeated in – an outlands waste where all hope falls on stony ground.

A desolate void where no roses grow.

For a while after that, I found myself drifting from job to job – nothing to do with journalism, just casual labour to keep me in booze. I stacked shelves for a while, did a couple of months on the buildings. But I always kept thinking of them walking through Dublin city, Imogen's face growing older every day. She would be seven next year, I would find myself thinking, as my stomach turned over violently. In the end I could bear it no longer. I woke up one day and knew I had no choice – I had to return. But, before I did that, I took myself on a trip to the seaside – down the coast to Bournemouth, to be precise.

When the woman on the coach asked me sympathetically:

—Why are you crying? Is there anything I can do to help?

I just shook my head and recounted to her what it had been like that first day we'd gone there. We'd brought Imogen to Bournemouth on a picnic.

—On the way home, I explained, she was so tired. But she said it was the best day of her life.

I looked away. My eyes were red-rimmed.

—I don't think I can go on without them, I said.

I made sure to say it to the hotel barman too, pretending to be drunker than I actually was.

—I'm glad you remember me, I said, for you won't be seeing me around again. It gets to the stage where life isn't worth it.

I didn't labour the point. Just gave enough information in order for him to remember when the police came inquiring.

At about four-thirty that morning I went down to the seafront. There wasn't a soul around – just this great big empty, impassive moon.

I deposited my pile of folded clothes at the water's edge, then turned around and simply walked away. In my head I could see the barman explaining, touchingly empathetic.

—His wife had just left him. Pity, that. They seemed such a happy couple the first time.

I knew they'd probably locate her too, the woman from the coach. That was all that was really necessary, I felt.

I didn't return to London. I caught a bus and headed for Wales. To Holyhead and the Rosslare ferry with nothing in my bag but a few bits of clothes, along with everything I'd collected about Ned Strange from the mountain.

I rented a bedsit in Portobello, on the south side of Dublin city, beside the canal, pragmatically – thankfully – using a false name, just in case things began to turn awkward. In the nights I'd stagger home from the pub and telephone these random numbers, rambling incomprehensibly about *The Snowman*, hanging up after hearing the voice of some confused and near-distraught housewife. It was stupid. I'm aware of that. But when you're wounded by betrayal, every single sinew in your body is stretched tight.

It's like at any moment you expect to detonate.

That was how I was feeling when, quite out of the blue, one day I picked up a copy of the *Sunday Independent* and found myself staring at a shockingly familiar face. It was Ned Strange. His photograph covered half the front page. I would be perturbed, to say the least, by what I was about to read. He had hanged himself, apparently, in the shower of Arbour Hill prison, while incarcerated there for the sexual abuse and murder of a young boy. I remembered the name and the minute I read it I went cold all over, and remembered the heart-warming words:

—I'm the bestest friend of Ned.

It was the little boy with the freckles who'd helped him feed his chickens: *Michael Gallagher!*

The subsequent account made me physically ill. To the extent that, when I had read the last sentence, I experienced this sense of some awful burden being lifted. As though the air all about me suddenly smelt sweeter. Just for having finished the thing. An irrational impulse impelled me to telephone Catherine, who was living in Rathfarnham now, to tell her about the horrific article. It was as though I felt it might elevate me in her eyes.

I became embarrassed then when I reflected on that thought, just standing blankly there on the landing, abstractedly clutching the Bakelite receiver.

I had a few drinks that Sunday, then went back to the bedsit when my money ran out. I'll never forget that day as long as

I live. All I remember is standing there on the landing – sensing instantly that something was wrong. The sodden smell began filling up my nostrils – the familiar choking odour of Olson's book *The Heart's Enchantment*. I dropped the keys and froze to the marrow when I heard his voice, the softest of whispers. I turned then and saw him, his heavy frame suffused with a pallid spectral light, standing there smoking in the embrasure of the window, staring blankly out across the city. He lowered the cigarette slowly and faced me, his lip curling with unmistakable disdain.

—You were going to phone her, weren't you? he sneered.

Then he did the oddest thing: smiled in a warm and affectionate way, as he opened his hand, revealing a small bar of chocolate. He extended his hand, offering it to me.

—I always like to bring a bar, he whispered mockingly, snapping off a square. Pushing it between his lips as he said:

—You've made a big mistake, Redmond. You just don't realise yet how big.

A few pieces of silver tinfoil fluttered to the floor as he drew in his breath and sucked his teeth in a parody of regret.

—It really is lovely, Redmond. You ought to have had some. You will though, you will one day.

I couldn't bear it. I wanted him to go. I was even prepared to abjectly plead:

—Please, Ned!

But when I looked again, he was gone and it was as though he had never been there. There was nothing but the curtain, blowing ever so gently.

Just wavering there in the gentle night breeze, as the last

faint wisps of the smoke wafted out into the moonlight, breaking up somewhere across the night city sky.

Whenever I'm walking by the canal, I'll often think of that night and just how debilitating, how emotionally draining it had been. It had affected me so deeply, not just for days afterwards but weeks, as I reproached myself constantly for my humiliating lack of resolve. The words 'Please, Ned!' returned to plague me – despite the fact that the occurrence was nothing more than a manifestation of my internal difficulties. I vowed never to return to that bedsit. I left without giving any notification, abandoning most of my possessions, apart from my 'folklore' papers regarding Ned.

I was fortunate enough to find a cheap place in a gentlemen's hostel, some miles away, across the river in Drumcondra. I know it seems rash but I never regretted it. It allowed me some space and some time in which to think. In retrospect, I think it was wise. Essential, even. There was nothing else I could realistically have done.

It's nothing to worry about, I'd persuade myself, such irrational perceptions are common, even predictable, in times of emotional turmoil. I'd persuade myself: It's just a symptom.

I couldn't afford for it to be anything else.

My lodgings as it turned out were streets ahead of the place in Portobello – bright and airy and, in fact, considerably cheaper. It was inconceivable to me that my previously highly strung state could possibly persist in surroundings which were so unthreatening and congenial and suited to my needs. That was how it, unquestionably, seemed. At last, I felt, I'd made a worthwhile decision.

Which is why, some nights later, I could have cried when I awoke with a start. The smell was in the room again – the very same damp and sickening smell. He raised the stogie slowly to his lips, standing there watching me at the end of the bed.

—Red, he whispered, I've come to ask you something. Do you remember that song I was playing the very first day you came? To Slievenageeha, I mean?

—Yes, I said.

—Did it mean anything to you?

I didn't understand. I shook my head. I could feel the cold sweat beginning to spread right across my body.

—No, I replied.

—No, he mimicked, quite bitterly.

He breathed in, then out.

—Do you even remember then what it was?

I had to confess I didn't. I couldn't think straight. I was overcome with trepidation.

—No, I repeated, almost shamefully.

His voice began to rise out of the still and silent gloom, as he delivered the song in the style of 'high lonesome'. It sounded hopelessly plangent, desperately lonely.

Here we both lie in the shade of the trees
My partner for ever just him and me
How long will we lie here O Lord who can tell?
Till the winter snow whitens the high hills of hell.

35

He remained silent for a long time afterwards. Then he said:

—Does it still mean nothing then, Redmond? Well, does it?

He shifted a little, sliding his hand deep into his pocket.

—I want to lie beside you, Redmond, he said.

He moved across the floor, edging closer to the bed.

—Would you like some chocolate, Redmond? Here, go on – have a bar.

He forced himself on me – there was nothing I could do. Had his way that awful night, flashing his incisors as he pressed the chocolate into my hand.

—There's a good boy, he said. Eat your chocolate for Uncle Ned.

The tinfoil pieces drifted to the floor as tears of shame came coursing down my cheeks.

Afterwards, he made it clear that it hadn't cost him a thought. He casually brushed the sweat from his forehead, buttoning his trousers with the wet stogie dangling from his lips.

—That will give you something to think about, my friend. And don't get ideas about reporting it to anyone. They'll only think it's your imagination. They'll say you're telling tales. Fanciful yarns like you'd hear on the mountain. So don't waste your time. Let's keep it between us – just you and me.

His eyes danced with roguish black mischief as he said:

—Here, this might help you. Prepare you for what is going to happen.

He threw something on to the table and was gone

without a sound. I climbed, trembling, from the bed. It was an old box camera photograph: a faded image of a little boy, standing in a hayfield on a sunny day, with the black cut-out of the mountain rising in the distance, crested by tall pines. He was smiling from ear to ear – a shock of red curls hanging down over his face. I flipped it in my hand and tried not to shiver as I read the words:

—For Little Red, the loveliest boy.

I found myself staring into my own eyes. It had been taken in the mountains many years before, when I was little more than eight years of age. My Uncle Florian's handwriting was barely legible now, after all the time that had passed. I couldn't wrench my gaze away. The damaged innocence and hope in those eyes reminded me of nothing so much as the expression of Michael Gallagher, the boy who'd trusted and treasured Ned Strange as a friend, only to find himself rewarded in the most horrific way imaginable – sexually assaulted, then brutally murdered. I found myself wishing I had never known Ned Strange. Had never gone near him, or had anything to do with him.

I didn't leave that room for days. I just kept waiting – knowing that sooner or later he'd return.

He didn't. All you could hear was the window rattling, and the sound of murmuring voices downstairs.

I carried the photograph everywhere with me now. I kept expecting to turn a corner and find him waiting, patiently raising the stogie to his lips. As he looked at me without flinching, stroking his beard with that chilling, teasing patience.

—Something dreadful is going to happen, Redmond, something really and truly dreadful. And when it happens, believe me, you'll *know*.

The streets were cluttered with stilt-walkers and jugglers – some protest to do with political prisoners. Drums pounded and bugles blared and an enormous papier mâché green and yellow caterpillar went curving past me, making its way in the direction of Mount Street.

At times, I'd find myself sitting in some café or half-empty pub, when, all of a sudden, a sensation of the deepest *alarm* would grip me, as though about to usher in an event of potentially deadly significance. To be classified into perpetuity as: *the disappearance of the photograph*!

A self-evidently illogical notion which, routinely, would manifest itself as folly when, almost numb with fear, I'd reach inside my pocket and locate it there within its folds, where it had been since morning, safe and secure.

I cannot begin to describe the immensity of the relief – triumph, even, which coursed through my body on such testing occasions.

I began, however, to fear that such impressions – erroneous though they might be – would soon begin to extend to all sorts of other areas. That I might, eventually, have to learn the whole world anew: so unfamiliar might things soon become. And there appeared to be no resources available to me to draw on to counter it. Adrift in a land of exaggerated hypotheses, I'd lean over the toilet bowl and get sick once more. Repeating like some meaningless mantra:

—I call myself Dominic Tiernan now but my name is actually Redmond Hatch. I'm Redmond Hatch and I live in Drumcondra. Drumcondra is in Dublin. I used to be married and I used to have a daughter. My daughter's name was Imogen and my wife's name was Catherine. Catherine and Imogen live in Dublin. They live in Dublin in Ireland in Europe. The road they live on is Ballyroan Road, Rathfarnham. I had found that out by calling up her sister and pretending she'd won a travel competition. It was devious, I know, something which might be expected from the likes of Ned Strange. But I had to do *something*!

I had to do *something*!

I couldn't believe it the first time I went out to Ballyroan, especially when I saw the little orchard out the back. I waited to see if Immy would come out. She didn't. I took a taxi to Rathmines and sat for hours in the Sunset Grill, trying to eat a Knickerbocker Glory. I couldn't. Then I went up to Cowper Road. It was awful, standing there looking in foolishly through the window – thinking of Catherine reading by the fire, listening to John Martyn as she serenely turned each page.

When we went to London first, Catherine and me, the life we lived was a kind of fairy tale, really. With your firstborn it's always different. You'll always hear people saying that. I can't comment, however, because – well, I'm never going to know about that now, am I?

No, I'll never know as we never got to have a second child. We had often talked about having a son. We had even extensively discussed his name. Owen he was going to be called. If he had ever managed to get born, that is. She said that things had changed between us. That my moods had altered with my lack of success. That she considered it somewhat risky – bringing a child into a situation that was unstable. Both financially and emotionally, she said. Giving me that look, which had become so familiar. Which once had said:

—I love you.

But now said:

—Now I'm not so sure.

But Christmas 1987, I remember as being really extra-special. Catherine had never looked more beautiful. In the rise of her bloom, as Ned had once remarked about Annamarie Gordon, when he'd told the story about her and him by the river. Where the two of them had gone on that precious day of *The Heart's Enchantment*.

Some of the things he said could really fool you – win you over and have you at his mercy.

—*The Heart's Enchantment*, he would say, abstractedly, that unique day of the heart's enchantment when I looked in her eyes and she looked in mine. When we knew we were going to be together for ever.

In the early days of marriage, it's like simple things, they've got this power to fill your entire heart full of love. After the initial débâcle with the *North London Chronicle*, Catherine could so easily have grumbled and moaned, and made things really very difficult indeed. But never – not once did I ever hear that woman complain. On special occasions, in Victoria Wine, they'd give her champagne or cigars as a perk.

—We live like kings, I remember her saying, around the time our ship started coming in, and I'd managed to get a few bits and pieces of freelancing. Too little, too late, as it turned out – but it seemed good then.

After a while, it gradually becoming clear that whatever difficulties we'd had, they were very soon going to be well and truly over.

It's still those early days I cherish most of all – the look on Imogen's face that Christmas Eve when I lifted her on to the carousel. She was four now. It was the most magnificent roundabout I'd ever laid eyes on – Russian or East European in style, painted in these gloriously elaborate swirling colours, with its herd of leaping horses and their fierce enamel grins.

I felt like the world had just begun as around and around I watched her turn, the light bulbs waltzing over Leicester Square as Santa urged his reindeers ever higher, his sleigh shimmering triumphantly somewhere beyond Admiral Nelson's hat.

Another magical time is the Saturday we discovered, to our complete astonishment, that a tax rebate had, just the day before, been credited to our account – to the princely tune of £2,000. I just stood there with my ATM card, staring blankly at the screen.

When I came to my senses, without hesitation, we whisked Imogen into Harrods' children's department and had her fitted for this lovely little coat, with a fur-trimmed collar and these great big buttons. She loved it. I never saw anything to compare with it, I swear.

She was a picture.

The Innocent: A Nation Mourns
The Lonely Death of Michael Gallagher

The report in the *Sunday Independent*, dated October 1989, had been truly unbearable. Describing how Ned had lured the boy away from Slievenageeha, betraying his trust in the most despicable way. It gave details of how he'd been regarded as Ned's 'little assistant', and in the photo he looked as sweet as an angel, completely oblivious of the true nature of his 'mentor'.

By all accounts, Strange had bribed him with a bar of chocolate, before driving him to a secluded spot on the outskirts of Dublin, near Blanchardstown. To a stream near a factory and a copse of pine. Under cover of which he intended to perpetrate his callous act.

You could see the factory in another photo – a grim, grey, functional building with the name ROHAN'S CONFECTION- ERY in the foreground. There was a description of the elevated ground and the thick pine-wooded area behind it, and the small winding river that ran close by. With a detailed account of how it had been coloured pinkish by the factory effluent, with the smell of spearmint 'thoroughly sickly' in the air, as though especially chosen 'for one evil purpose'.

I lowered my head and prayed softly for Michael Gallagher, his precious life snuffed out by a duplicitous, self-serving pervert.

A man I'd once known by the name of Ned Strange.

Renewed revulsion began welling up within me when I thought of how I too had been so cunningly deceived. And – actually *tolerated it*!

He had been amusing himself with me right from the beginning, making up stupid stories in so-called mountain language – old-time phrases which probably never, at any time, possessed any authentic currency. He gradually came to symbolise for me everything I'd ever resented about the mountain, reminding me why I'd fled from it the very first chance I got.

It made me uncomfortable even thinking about it. Thinking that I'd been born there – in Slievenageeha or anywhere near it.

A place – as has so often been observed about such places – where the inhabitants never looked you in the eye, where everything they did seemed sly and calculated. It was as if everything they represented was to be found in him, Ned Strange: hospitable, certainly, but never, under any circumstances, to be trusted.

There was, you always suspected, a self-aggrandising purpose to everything they did, a callous selfishness ever-present in their shady, dirt-poor, suspicious, backward hearts.

*   *   *

43

I was sorry now I had ever returned there, to compile an article on folklore or anything else. And was embarrassed beyond words by the more sympathetic things I'd written about it in the past, lamely seduced by Ned Strange's honeyed words and my own dishonest, rose-tinted memories, many of which I still retained, stuffed in a folder back in the hostel, including the manuscript of our proposed 'story of his life'.

I couldn't bear to think about them now.

Enchanted Days: Courtship in the Ireland of Long Ago by Redmond Hatch

(*Leinster News*, 9 April 1982)

When Red Ned Strange, or Auld Pappie as he is affectionately known in his home place of Slievenageeha, was a young man in his early twenties, he met and fell in love with a young girl by the name of Annamarie Gordon. Annamarie's father was long since dead and she lived on a farm with a few cattle and her mother. It was quite by chance that those two young people encountered one another one day at the fair. Ned at the time was quite a shy young man and it took a lot to ask her out walking, as was the custom at the time. But ask her he did and they were soon boon companions. And rarely a day would go past without them wandering — along the valley and off down by the river. These were the sort of things they used to say to one another:

—I'll love you till the ends of the earth.

And:

—You're my darling, my loving sweetheart for all time.

Ned Strange is a virtuoso musician – a fiddle-player without peer, whose renditions of 'The Pride of Erin' and 'Strip the Willow' are legendary in this part of the world. He is fascinating company and an incomparable storyteller and repository of local history. He is an absolute delight to converse with and his heart-warming reminiscences are uplifting in an age that has seemed to have forgotten the value of such storytelling skills – if not indeed abandoned them altogether. While Mr Strange is around, the spirit of the ceilidh – by which I mean the good neighbourliness and fellowship which our fathers and grandfathers knew so well – I am pretty much sure will never be lost.

Good health to him and all his noble generation!

1990

Two: Where the Wild Things Are

I WAS WALKING ONE day by the Royal Canal. I do that often. I haven't worked since the night he came, that dreadful night in the Portobello bedsit. I keep thinking of his eyes: those loathsome, lustful, self-serving eyes. That caliph smile.

For a while I tried – I got a job in Supermac's, a fast food outlet on Drumcondra Road. But I got the customer's change wrong on a number of occasions and in the end they had no option, I was told, but to release me.

It was nothing personal – that was just the way things were. In a way, I was relieved: it gave me a lot more time to think, to root out all impediments and obstacles and clear in my mind an unobstructed path towards the future – and, with a bit of luck, a whole new life.

I was walking along the towpath of the canal one day when two street people, I suppose you might call them – or maybe more precisely, junkies – approached me, position- ing themselves somewhat oppressively on either side.

They began making demands with various veiled threats. For watches, money, this and that. I gave them what I had – which wasn't much, predictably. And which, they soon made clear, they didn't consider sufficient.

They then insisted that I turn out my pockets.

I hadn't slept the whole night before and I'd been thinking of Imogen riding around on the carousel. So I just said:

—No. I can't do that.

The box camera photo was still in my pocket. And, more than anything, I didn't want that taken. It was the only one from those days which wasn't *vile*. It was all I had. I did my best to explain that to them.

But that, evidently, provided them with little more than a source of amusement. One of them even laughed aloud, as a matter of fact, before brushing threateningly against my shoulder.

—Just fucking give it, will you, one of them – even more menacingly now – suggested, don't go making things hard on yourself.

Life is so cruel – full of these chance, random encounters.

I read about the incident in the evening paper the following day. The taller one was wearing a hood, shrinking from the camera as he related his story. You could just about make out the bandage, masking the deep wound I'd inflicted on his face. He went on at length about how I'd done this and how I'd done that . . .

Things I had neither done nor contemplated.

I didn't read as far as the end.

*　　*　　*

Catherine had always planned to come back to Ireland – to get herself the house with the orchard. How many times we'd imagined Imogen in that, just playing away in a world of her own.

That was our dream when we came home.

As I say, they live in Rathfarnham now. In common with so many other places in Dublin, it's been utterly transformed, with swirling concrete motorway intersections and endlessly pounding, remorseless traffic. The city seems blighted, almost out of control: the carnage on the roads continues as though some inconsequential, diverting carnival. You are hunted in and out of shops, glared at by security men bloated on steroids. Old-timers haunt the fringes of the city, afraid to penetrate its boundaries lest they be set upon by the young: arraigned and made to give an account of themselves. Much of the time I'll travel alone. Spend hours, perhaps, drifting on a bus. I feel at home in its bright, insulated interior. As though it were a link with former, less complicated times. As I travel onwards, going nowhere in particular. Sometimes I'll go out to Cowper Road, or just sit in the Sunset Grill.

Drifting onwards, jostled, directed – skitting like a steel ball through the polished and brightly coloured channels of the new city-machine, my ears ringing with the sound of sirens and engines, pneumatic drills and sweeping cranes and the transatlantic beat of the new lingua franca, the patois of schoolchildren and businessmen indistinguishable now, rising as it does in bursts from the pavements – past twenty-four-hour shopping malls, asphalt grids and multi-storey car parks, takeout delis, convention hotels, brass-and-glass bank doors and multiplex cinemas, hurtling now towards some amorphous, haphazard future.

It's not like the city I knew at all. The young can have it. I'm not young any longer. It's a long time since I felt that way. I know a lot of people might think that the age difference between me and Catherine – having been born in 1941, I was twenty years older – was significant. But anyone who thinks that – well, I've got news for them.

They're wrong. It had nothing to do with it at all. I asked her.

—I didn't even notice, she told me. All I noticed were your cute copper curls.

Imogen anyway used to make me feel young. Once I caught this old woman staring at us, shaking her head in disbelief as the pair of us played together in Queen's Park, pretending the whole park had been turned into Ponyville from *My Little Pony*. I think the old lady thought we were being too noisy. But I didn't care. That's how, you see, Imogen could make you feel. I emitted this whinny and the old woman winced.

—Giddy-up! Imogen said and chucked the imaginary reins. Giddy-up now, Kimono!

—All right, Pinkie Pie!

Pinkie Pie was a sweet lamb of a pony who loved to try all these new fun things but sometimes could get just that little bit nervous. Sometimes Immy liked playing at being her because she liked me comforting her when the 'afraid' things were over. There was no evidence of anything frightening her now. No 'afraid' things at all as she chucked on Kimono's reins.

—Giddy-up! I told you, you bad pony, Kimono!

After playing *My Little Pony* we went to Burger King where we both had Bacon Doubles which we loved. That was what we always had there – and we promised not to tell Catherine, for she'd always said that it wasn't food at all. That it was full of starch and additives and everything. I would have given anything for one of them now, one specially made in Burger King in Kilburn, as I drifted aimlessly through the streets of Dublin city.

There is a pub across the road and I can see their house from there. I've seen Catherine a number of times. The very first time – it was hard. It was unbearable, actually, to tell the truth. Imogen goes to the Holy Faith Convent now.

Not long after Catherine began studying in Willesden College, whenever little things I'd done had got on her nerves a bit, she'd start these arguments. Especially if she was a little tipsy or in any way intoxicated. You could often find them erupting then.

—Do you ever think you might have a problem with women, Redmond? A sort of old-fashioned, almost back-woods tendency? That you might tend to idealise them a little in your mind? That somehow, in your mind, they're either angels or . . .

I don't remember her finishing that sentence. She didn't have to – I knew what she meant. I could see why some things about me might have annoyed her – but that one I never could quite understand. Because any time I looked at her or Imogen, that was all I could see.

The most beautiful angels in all of Christendom.

'Whores' is the word she didn't use in that sentence. She meant: do you think of other women as whores? If she'd said it I'd have answered her 'no'.

Because I didn't, you see, think of any other women. Never had and never wanted to. I had all the women I needed at home. Although, like Ned had often pointed out, it would have been nice to have had a son. It would have been nice to have been given the opportunity. But that's no excuse to raise your hand to your wife. Which Ned had done.

I know because he told me.

Catherine's partner works in finance. He works in the Financial Services Centre in the centre of town. When I'm feeling down, I've this urge to imagine that Catherine has gone to seed.

It isn't true, however.

I've heard it suggested that certain women have this quality – that they become more attractive as they get older. Kind of more refined, and . . . *classy*, or something. I don't know. I can't say for sure. But if anyone has, it's Catherine Courtney. She didn't stay with her Maltese friend. I don't know why. I don't know any of the details. All I know is, they broke up very shortly after coming back to Dublin. He didn't like Ireland I think. And after a while Catherine met someone else.

I wonder does she ever mention him to her new partner?

I wonder does she tell him that her and the Maltese made love every Wednesday?

While I was trudging the wet streets of London, collecting rejected articles, dreaming of having another baby with her, racking my brains trying to come up with ideas for features that might make us some money.

—Owen, I'd sigh, as I strolled along.

While she was attending her 'Women's Studies' classes which were held in Willesden three nights a week. After which she attended her 'Maltese' class.

I wonder does she ever mention *that* to Ivan?

I wonder does she ever mention *me*?

Renewed football fever saw the city deserted. Ireland were playing Albania in the World Cup qualifiers, so the radio said. Papers blew idly, alarm bells lingered emptily. It was like the aftermath of a neutron bomb. I'd try not to think at all about Strange.

Not to mention what he'd *done*.

I almost vomited when I thought of it.

Then I'd have a few drinks and realise how absurd it all was – sitting in a pub, considering what effectively were mere symptoms, by-products of stress.

—Ghosts! I'd laugh.

In a modern city in the middle of the day. It was ludicrous.

—Ned! I'd hear myself chortle. For Christ's sake Redmond – I mean Dominic – what are you bloody well talking about!

And that would do the trick. I would almost feel like I'd returned to normal. The way I used to be when I first started work – a happy, carefree man in my early twenties: full of faith and belief in the world and the possibility of all sorts of wonderful and terrific things happening. I'd meet some football fans and we'd have ourselves a laugh. Once I got drunk with a crowd of them and had myself a real whale of a time, twirling an Irish scarf and shouting 'Ole Ole Ole!' as brazenly and exuberantly as the rest of them. I remember sneering in the middle of it all:

—He's a lying fucking pervert, and that's all he ever was! Only an idiot like me would ever have tolerated it, him and his fucking obnoxious manipulations!

If he'd appeared at that moment, I remember thinking, I'd have been more than capable of standing up to him. Of flagrantly scorning him, even, standing there laughing as he slunk away shamefully – thereby revealing his true nature.

For Ned Strange was nothing, and *had* never been anything but a coward. I knew that for sure now and he didn't cost me a thought. I had stopped even thinking about him now, to tell the truth.

—A by-product of stress is all he is! I cried, much to the amusement of some of the revellers. Stress, boys – that's all it was!

In the small hours of the following morning, that, however, was not how it seemed at all. I found myself waking, cold and shivering, with the curtains bellying silently in the windows. It was only after a minute or so that I realised the glass had actually come in. It lay scattered in shards all over

56

the floor. I knew I ought to have called on the caretaker to fix it, but the drink had got to me and the more I thought about that the less I could face it.

In the end I just stuck a cardboard box up against it and did my best to get back to sleep. It didn't work.

I got up and paced the floor for an hour. I flicked through an old magazine. There was an article inside about the beauty of Yugoslavia, from way back some time in the fifties. It seemed like somewhere close to Paradise and you have no idea how I envied the tiny beach figures disporting themselves in that Kodachrome dream. I'd do my best to lose myself in it but every so often my eyes, in spite of me, would veer towards the door. Convincing myself I'd heard someone on the landing. Which, fortunately, in the end, I succeeded in persuading myself was just silly.

It sounded so *stupid*.

I raised my head and confidently sniffed the air. Not a whiff of soddenness, dampness or anything else. Not a sign that Ned Strange was in the building or anywhere even near it. The ideas you get into your head, I thought.

It was hard not to laugh when you thought of it now, how illogical you could be in times of personal difficulty. After all the agitation, in the end I slept like a top. Didn't wake up until well after twelve.

Nonetheless, just to be on the safe side, I went to the doctor and he gave me some sleeping tablets.

—I'll give you Diphenhydramine HCI, 25 mg. Take two every night.

—Thank you, I said, thinking about The Unicorn. That was the restaurant Ivan and her ate in. I'd seen them going in there a number of times.

The doctor cast me a patronising smile and off I went about my business. I took the tablets – but they weren't any good. I lost track of time and became even more – if it were possible – fearful and dislocated. That was the main reason that I turned to religion. I just couldn't stand it any longer. There was a church I knew in Harold's Cross. I started going there every day. Looking for someone – anyone – who'd do what the tablets hadn't succeeded in doing. Regulate my life – dispel this pervasive, all-consuming uncertainty. Take me into their comforting arms. I thought that maybe Jesus would do it. I discovered, however, that I was wrong. Jesus was lazy. He took too many things for granted. It was like he was thinking: It's enough just to be here. To sit on the cross doling out would-be sympathetic looks. While you yourself did all the work. It wasn't enough, I'm afraid. I'm sorry, but it simply wasn't enough for me.

Nobody bothers with religion any longer. Huddled shapes raggedly, sparsely embroider the black depths of the cloisters, idling outside by the rainswept granite gables, shambling about like they're already dead. Stray mongrels loiter aimlessly by the rusty churchyard gates, drooping moss clings to ancient defeated Marian shrines. Clergymen appear weighed down by guilt, shuffling obsequiously through streets, full of shame. A lot of them have been convicted of the same crime as Strange.

The priest I dealt with was kind, considerate. But he

looked drained and impossibly tired. Somewhat abstractedly, he informed me that persistence was all I required. Persistence and time, he assured me, smiling unconvincingly. I felt sorry for him, but still drifted out in the middle of his homily.

It was a windswept day on Harold's Cross Road. The rain was blowing in swathes towards the city as I stood there clinging to the churchyard railings, my entire body shuddering violently, tears mingling with raindrops as they coursed down my face.

—Be mindful that, having exercised your will contrary to that of God and chosen iniquity, you alone will be responsible for the consequences! I heard and became afraid.

But in the end I didn't care. I knew I no longer had any choice. I simply had nowhere else to go.

—Yes! I cried. And yes again!

A woman was observing me. I glared at her: Don't dare come near me!

I was lathered in sweat. Thick saliva had gathered on my lips. I felt like turning and spitting at the church. Extremes of heat and cold went surging through me, warm blood cascading from my nostrils.

—Redmond, I heard, softly whispered on the wind, you know you can trust me. I'll look after you. Till the very last pea is out of the pot, till the angels quit the hallowed halls of heaven.

For the first time in years I felt that I belonged.

—Thank you, I answered happily, as my voice was

carried off on the breeze and I applied the sodden crimson hankie to my face.

Contrary to what might have been expected in the circumstances, finding myself in a state of what can only be described as near-delirium.

When I looked again the woman was gone, the bus plashing onwards towards the golden, lit-up city.

All that summer I prayed and prayed, to one I now knew in my heart wouldn't fail me. A reassuring lightness had entered my heart and I gradually began to feel the enormous weight lifting from my shoulders. I was so grateful I cannot begin to tell you. It was such a dramatic renewal of the spirit that I found myself gradually beginning to give serious consideration to the possibility that one day Catherine and I might actually get back together again.

Even to the extent of composing a letter:

> To Catherine and Imogen, from Redmond, your ever-loving husband and father. For the first time today I found myself thinking: maybe we'll leave the outlands behind. Maybe we'll come back to the place that together we knew so well. Do you think that might happen, Imogen? Maybe you'd ask your darling mother.

I don't know exactly why I scribbled out 'father' when I was signing the letter. Scored it out and pencilled in 'Auld Pappie'. It just seemed such a natural thing to do, really, much more representative of the emotions I was feeling: I wanted to be warm and secure and tender, and to let her

60

know exactly how things were. I wanted her to call me Pappie, you see. Also it was a definitive way of bidding goodbye at long last to my so-called 'visitor'. Something that was definitely a long time overdue. Ridding myself of him by becoming a profound exemplar of a father – and not some foul and abhorrent pederast the likes of him. There was only one place he and his ilk belonged – in the outlands. That desert of the spirit which had been expressly created for men like Ned Strange. In the barren fields where no roses would ever grow. Where even the *idea* of a flourishing rose would be unthinkable. I thought of him: wide-eyed and naked and covered in crimson blotches, standing by his window looking out to see if he could see Michael Gallagher. His trembling lips parting as he whispered:

—Why, it's Michael. Look, my little friend – I've got some chocolate here in my pocket. Have a piece. Take it from Ned.

It was disgusting even to have to speak his name.

When we were in bed, Catherine would often smile and run her fingers through my hair.

—You really don't know how much I love you, do you?

I'd say no – and look away, a little embarrassed. Even though we were married I still could be a little shy like that.

—Redmond Hatch – my own Little Red. You can look so handsome, at times, you know.

I'd still say nothing and she'd peck me on the cheek. Then she'd lean over and kiss my neck softly.

—Do you know how much I love you, Red? Till the seas

run dry, till the mountains crumble. That's how much I love you, Redmond. That's how much I love you – you and your sweet little sugar lips. Till the very last pea is out of the pot. 'Sugar lips'. I loved it. It was our own special 'making love' name. Nobody had ever loved *him* like that. Strange, I mean. Nobody had ever said anything like that to *him*. All he could get was a child to abuse. Nobody had ever loved him – ever. And never would. Not now.

Till Slievenageeha Mountain crumbled to the sea, till the winter snow whitened the high hills of hell.

As I folded the writing paper and sealed the envelope, I was consumed from head to toe by a warm and comforting *safe* kind of glow. I could just imagine Imogen looking up as she said:

—Can we go to winterwood now, Pappie? The Snow Princess – she'll be there.

I was just on my way out to post the letter when, suddenly, I experienced this truly appalling *crawling* sensation.

I stood stock-still in the centre of the landing. I could hear it – the sound of breathing at regular intervals. A massive shadow, misshapen and elongated, was slowly forming in the far corner of the room.

—So, that was your special 'making love' name, was it? I wonder did she ever call *him* that?

There could be no mistaking his taunting chuckles.

—Leave me alone! *Do you hear me?* I pleaded. I thought you promised – you said I could *trust* you!

*   *   *

As it happened, it turned out to be nothing at all. Nothing but the wind, blowing desultorily through a loosely plastered crevice, round about the size of a medium-sized coin.

I was considerably cheered by that – the idiotic innocence of it, in a way. A fact which may well have been evident later when I was purchasing cigarettes. The shop assistant was displaying similarly buoyant feelings. The Republic, she told me, had performed like titans on the playing field again.

—You have to hand it to the boys in green, she beamed.

—It's a great day, I smiled.

And it was – the more I reflected on my ludicrous 'imaginings'.

—It is indeed, she agreed, it most certainly is.

The football tournament held little interest for me, to be honest. But I was gratified, nonetheless, on her account – and that of all the others who had begun to stream from the pubs and clubs, clamorously regaining the streets once more. An indisputable equanimity had now, at last, settled over my soul – and I simply can't emphasise to you enough just how grateful I was for that.

Which explains why I became so dispirited that very evening on my return to the hostel. I had been actually whistling as I was coming across the landing – when I heard myself crying out:

—Jesus!

There could be no mistaking it this time – it was there

again. The *dampness*, that awful familiar asphyxiating *odour*, exactly the same as that very first night, when he'd stood by the window in a tortuous silence. I was so frightened by the thought of what might be about to happen that my limbs refused to respond. I couldn't speak. It was a long time before I regained my strength.

And when at last I did – with an enormous sense of relief, believe me – I began scouring the floorboards of the landing. High and low, on my knees, examining each individual one.

In spite of my best efforts, failing to come up with anything of significance. I could find no indication, none at all, of any disturbance.

And stood there in vain trying to comprehend what had happened.

I had definitely locked the door, I remembered locking it earlier on. But now – it was *wide open*!

I stood there, baffled, tears of frustration starting from my eyes.

It took me some time to get over that episode, for no explanation I could come up with seemed in any way to satisfactorily explain it. The same was applicable to my enquiries within the hostel itself. In retrospect, it would have been better if I'd stopped drinking for a while. It would have been better if I hadn't gone to the pub in Rathfarnham. But it's easy to say that now. It's just unfortunate it happened to be located directly across the road from Catherine's house.

I think that what happened was, I had been watching the

match being relayed on a massive video screen when I looked up and saw Catherine's partner Ivan standing directly across the road. Laughing and joking with the hedge-clippers in his hand. When I saw him laughing like that – beaming away and passing the clippers to Imogen – I have to admit that for the very first time I began to feel just the tiniest measure of sympathy for 'Auld Pappie' and the dreadful things that had happened to him over the years. Or, maybe if not sympathy exactly, then perhaps, for the first time, just the smallest, tiniest *glimmer* of empathy. Certainly, finding myself considerably more comprehending than I'd previously been. Much more so than at any time since the very first night of the—

I can't bring myself even to *utter* the word 'assault'.

When, out of nowhere, he'd uttered these oddly moving words:

—Why was love denied to me, Redmond? Why was I denied a son? A son I would have loved and who would have loved me in return? It isn't fair, Redmond.

With devastating tenderness, to my amazement, he had continued:

—I knew your mother, you know, Little Red. That's what she used to call you, isn't it?

I felt like crying when I heard him saying that. Thinking of my photo and how I'd pretended my mother had taken it. Had taken that photo of what an ordinary child was supposed to look like. That proper *likeness* of a properly loved boy, who didn't do things like dance hornpipes for his uncle, behind tall trees or anywhere else.

*　　*　　*

All children are beautiful but you always think your own's the best. That's what I thought the first day I saw Imogen.

I sat there in the pub, sipping away at my tepid pint of ale. I stared at them in the garden, snipping away at the roses. Imogen was holding a basin of flowers and smiling. A shaft of sunlight lit up the bar's interior as a roar of triumph went up for Ireland. A supporter in a giant green hat dropped his trousers and bared his buttocks. Nobody noticed. Too immersed in the action replay.

When I came home that evening, initially I had been in good humour, but, to my dismay, that now familiar invasive feeling of *imminence* began to grow, even stronger than before. And no amount of reasoning could seem to dispel it.

I knew Imogen had her lunch break in the Holy Faith at one o'clock so I made sure to arrive there good and early. I was amazed at myself for having taken the decision but was more than gratified by the feeling of self-worth it had – quite unexpectedly – generated inside of me.

Obviously I was taking a risk – but just seeing her once, I knew, would make it worthwhile. Officially, of course, I was barred from having any contact with her – without prior written approval from her mother. Which, for one reason or another, obviously, wouldn't be forthcoming. The truth is, she had concocted a number of stories to make me look bad. Ned Strange had been quite a master at that in his time – embellishing the truth to suit his own ends. But he was nothing to Catherine Courtney whenever she got going.

The mind-bogglingly elaborate narratives she could come up with when she had to – they really were quite astonishing. Involving, as they did, 'violent scenes' and 'obscenities'. Not to mention the various 'not-so-veiled threats', with which she'd been preoccupied in the court-room. Also 'insane jealousies' and 'over-protective neuroses'.

Baby Owen, of course, wasn't even mentioned, or any of the arguments connected with that issue. I told the judge that I regretted a lot of my behaviour – especially the sudden irrational rages. I had just wanted us all to be the happiest family ever, but, unfortunately, things hadn't developed that way. Catherine said under no circumstances could she countenance having another child – we were much too unstable, financially and emotionally. I said that was a pity. Catherine, however, didn't say anything. Things gradually went from bad to worse. Whole weeks would go by and we wouldn't exchange a word. Then it happened, that incident in the bedroom, pathetically turning a polly pocket in my hand.

It would be better for everyone if I didn't see the child, the judge had ultimately concluded, outside of the conditions which she would now lay down. That was her ruling, mystifying though it might have been, as Imogen just stood there, pale and bewildered.

In my days of regular employment I would never have dreamt of doing such a thing. However I categorically admit it – I stole the book.

I didn't have any choice. I had to have a present for

Immy. It was called *Where the Wild Things Are* by Maurice Sendak. It really has to be said that there were some fabulous creatures depicted within its colourfully illustrated pages. Extraordinarily intimidating but somehow attractive creations, dragons and sprites and other denizens of Middle-earth. Its audaciously extravagant draughtsmanship cheered me no end. Not to mention the sheer impish glee of the stories themselves. There could be no doubt, I thought to myself, that the author, when it came to imagination, stood head and shoulders above them all, in the world of children's fiction at least. Immy had always loved that book. I thought that maybe when I picked her up we might go and read it together in the park. Leafing through it on the bus, the thing that struck me most impressively was how it seemed every bit as fresh and original now as that first night we'd read it together, in her bedroom.

As she lay there sucking her thumb in the glow of the night light that Catherine had bought.

In Camden market when she'd loved me.

I was so excited waiting for the school bell outside the convent. Except that it never came. Which, of course, deep down I knew. It was the school's day off. I had only been pretending to pick her up. It was stupid, I know, a childish thing to do. But I got so giddy when I thought of it. The doors bursting open and Immy crying:

—Daddy!

I could see the cleaner passing by the school window, looking up intermittently and lugubriously gazing out, as though utterly perplexed by the strange world beyond.

I would have given anything to go to the pub. But I didn't have any money and wasn't due to get the dole until Thursday. So I just started walking back towards the hostel and Drumcondra. I was crossing the canal bridge when the fear came over me and I found myself just standing there. The voice came drifting thinly to my ears.

—That was a very stupid thing you did, Redmond, you don't want anyone to know you are in Dublin. Don't ever do a thing like that again.

I lowered my head in abject humility.

—Yes, of course. Yes, of course, I know, I replied and resumed my journey in the echo-specked dusk.

It just wasn't enough for me. To be told, like a child, when it would be acceptable for me to see my daughter. It made me sick even thinking about it. I could hear her saying:

—Why does it have to be this way? Is there any reason for it, Daddy?

—None that I can think of, darling. None that I can think of in the wide, wide world, Imogen, my beloved pet.

I sat in the common room for a couple of hours, turning the pages of *Where the Wild Things Are*.

—Oh no! I'd hear my sweetheart say, recoiling from some big scaly dragon or other, pressing her fists up to her face as the lovely glow of the night light burnt on.

1991

Three: My Little Pony

I WAITED IN TEMPLE BAR, knowing they'd come by sooner or later. I won't pretend it didn't shock me when it happened though. I knew the restaurant. We'd frequented it together, once upon a time. But it wasn't called Rudyard's now – it was a pasta place, where they ate alfresco, an indication of what was to come, the Temple Bar area developing into the epicentre of Dublin's hedonistic empire, a playground exclusively populated by louche adolescent Euro-ramblers and indigenous chemical-fuelled youths vertiginously wading in the currents of an ever-expanding opalescent ocean, shorn of history and oblivious of religion. It was a bright evening – fresh and crisp. A forlorn mime artist was half-heartedly juggling coloured balls close by the Central Bank. Imogen was wearing this sparkly top with a heart-shaped bag thrown across her shoulder. She was nine now, and wore her hair in a ponytail. She was holding her father's hand as she chatted, non-stop, as usual. The seagulls seemed to blow like random flecks of saliva. It was too much to deal with, no matter how much I thought I had prepared myself for it. I had to have a drink – one. That was all I had the money for. It failed miserably to fortify me.

I stood in the alleyway across the street from the restaurant. As I looked in the window, the sight saddened me so much I can't find the words which might adequately describe it. Imogen was throwing her head back with her fists up to her face, laughing away at some joke he had told. In front of her on the table was a Knickerbocker Glory. Her father was helping her to eat it. I watched her sink in her long-handled spoon, right into the middle of that great big multicoloured ice cream mountain. Her new father was wearing a casual diamond-patterned jumper. My vision became somewhat blurred as I stood there in the cobbled alleyway, with streams of people sweeping past me. I heard something about the Temple Bar Music Centre. John Martyn was playing there, a girl said in passing. 'May you never,' I heard her sing. Another song that Catherine had loved – 'May you never lay your head down without a hand to hold.'

Imogen had always been crazy about pizza. Every Sunday I'd bring her to Deep Pan, close by our flat, which was on Lonsdale Road in Kilburn. She'd cry: 'Pineapple – yay!' and Catherine would say: 'It's salami for me!'

After they left the restaurant, I was still a little unsteady, not yet wholly back to myself. But I managed to keep them in sight. They caught a taxi on Aungier Street. People will tell you there's no such thing as real coincidence. That synchronicity etc. is just so much waffle. But it did seem remarkably strange to me that scarcely five minutes later, after the taxi had pulled away and after dazedly wandering into a shop, the first thing I came upon happened to be a video of *My Little Pony*. And not just any old copy of it either, but the very one I remembered watching with Immy – *The Enchanted Mask*, in fact. Where Rainbow Dash, Minty and Wisteria are going to the magic castle with Sunny Daze. I remembered it especially because Pinkie Pie wasn't in it and Immy had been very disappointed by that. My heart was thumping furiously from the moment I saw it. It started me thinking about Imogen and her toys. I can't tell you how excited she used to get about all those ponies and their crazy adventures in Ponyville: the two of us singing the theme song in Queen's Park – Imogen being Pinkie Pie and me being Kimono.

—Do the 'afraid' things, she'd say and I'd scare her.

Pinkie Pie was the 'scarediest' pony.

'Boo!' could even qualify as a scary thing for her.

But she always loved it when the time came to comfort her. When the scary things were all over at last.

—They won't come back, will they, the 'afraid' things? she'd say.

—Of course they won't, Pinkie Pie, I'd tell her.

—Can we watch it again? she would say when the video at last had come to an end.

And I'd say, real cross:

—No! You know you've watched it twice already, Immy! I would not.

—You certainly can, Pinkie Pie! I'd say and laugh my head off.

75

I'd have let her watch it a hundred times if she'd wanted. A hundred and fifty.

She could watch the video till the tape wore away as far as her father was concerned.

It just used to floor me the way that girl could giggle, with her little shoulders rocking back and forth. Then we'd have ourselves a glass of Ribena. She always liked one before she went to bed. But I never told Catherine – because I knew she'd go mad. She didn't like her drinking it at all. Additives, and so on.

It was our little secret, I told Imogen to remember.

—Our little secret, she chuckled, 'The Secret of Ribena'!

In the common room of the hostel you had permission to watch videos after 6 p.m., provided no one else objected. When I went in there was nobody else around. Just this one fellow, a rough-looking labourer, jowly, in his mid-fifties. When I asked him did he mind if I put on *The Enchanted Mask* he said no.

As a matter of fact he watched it with me.

—They're sortae like the Care Bears, aren't they, mate? he suggested. Same type o' thing – right?

He was from Glasgow, he told me. He was correct. Sunny Daze and Rainbow Dash and all the rest *were*, in fact, very similar to the Care Bears. With all the action taking place in this incorrigibly pink, totally candyfloss world. About halfway through I heard him asking me some questions about the football match but he didn't persist when I demonstrated no interest.

Later on he told me he'd been working on the oil rigs for years. Before things – well, went wrong, he said.

—I worked on Piper Alpha, he said. I was asleep down below the night she went up. I'll no' forget it. Tell ye the truth, I've no' been the same since. I seen flames that night 300 feet high.

He was very interested when he heard I'd once worked for a newspaper. He asked me would I be interested in hearing his life story? Maybe write it up: 'The Inside Story of Piper Alpha'. But he said he had lots of stories to tell. Not just depressing, awful ones like that.

I was in no humour for hearing anyone's story. I'd had my fill of stories. In any case, I had my suspicions that he'd never been near Piper Alpha at all. That, like Strange, he nurtured this image of himself as some unique, great trailblazing adventurer. When he'd probably, in fact, been living in dosshouses for years.

I told him I'd see him later and left.

A couple of nights later my sleep was interrupted by the sound of a street party, with a boombox thumping away outside, the piercing whistles and pounding drums seeming to wane before resurging with a renewed vigour that seemed not just invasive but deeply provocative, in fact. The perspiration was running off me as I got up, although the weather hadn't been particularly hot. I went down to the communal kitchen to get myself a glass of water and was scooping some ice cubes into the glass when I heard the kitchen door suddenly slam. I dropped the glass. Then froze as I heard:

—Bastard! Fucking bastard!

At that point, I could have sworn I smelt the loathed dampness.

—O Jesus, I groaned, as I glimpsed my face in the window. It was chalk-white.

—Bastard! the oil-rigger repeated, before launching into an unnecessary torrent of vile invective. My relief – when I realised who it was, and also, of course, who it *wasn't* – was immense. Piper Alpha stood before me, quaking. It gradually emerged that he had been bitterly aggrieved by my earlier reluctance to lend what he described as 'a sympathetic ear' to his experiences.

I had no option but to persuade him that he'd been mistaken. Which he hadn't. His appraisal of the situation had been, in fact, entirely accurate. I *hadn't* been listening to his tiresome 'life story'. Not to a single word he'd said. But I made us some tea to mollify the cretin. We sat together at the table. He must have been droning on for at least three hours. Eventually, his eyelids began to droop.

—I think that's enough for tonight, don't you think so, Dominic, my friend? he said as he stood up and pushed back the table. Adding, charmingly: I thought at first you were a bit of a cunt, but now I think you're all right.

Catherine used to say:

—You can be canny, can't you, Redmond Hatch? Quite resourceful when it serves your purpose? Not at all the innocent you like to pretend. Must be your rural background. That old native cunning we often hear about.

I smiled at the recollection of my wife's tender ways.

Then I heard Piper Alpha bidding me goodnight, shambling off, suitably placated.

As I stood there, out of nowhere, I experienced this appalling image of Imogen – screaming on Piper Alpha as the oil-rigger cried:

—She'll be burnt alive!

It was as though she were there in that hostel kitchen. Right there screaming and begging me for help.

—The afraid things! The afraid things, Daddy!

Why, I asked myself, ought I to think of such a thing? What had prompted me to—

Then I saw her again: a silhouetted dwarf behind a ragged fence of fire. Her arms reaching out in tortured appeal.

—Ah, I heard a familiar voice whisper, have you gone and lost your precious little friend? I lost mine too. He drowned one day, in the sweet factory river.

I went back to bed but, once again, sleep proved impossible. I couldn't stop imagining Imogen in Bournemouth. She was wearing this daft little floral bikini and every time Ivan shouted she raced along the shore to the water. And stood like she used to, pressing her fists up to her face. I wondered had Ivan ever actually brought her to the seaside? Ivan, in so far as I had been able to make out, was a very good father. He definitely spent a lot of time with her. Assisting her with her lessons and, generally, being as dutiful as he could. I thought of Catherine lying there on the Bournemouth sand. Removing her sunglasses and looking over as she said:

—If I didn't love you, I'd marry John Martyn. I'd marry him and call him 'sugar lips'.

I found myself laughing, exactly as I'd done back then.

—'May You Never', I had said to her with a chuckle.

Once she had actually said she'd got married too young and that she hadn't really lived her life fully. That she liked being – *adored*, certainly. What woman didn't? But only up to a point. She wanted to be loved for herself, she said. I wondered had they discussed it in the classes? All I knew was – it hadn't bothered her before. And it made me sad. Because, deep down, I couldn't seem to stop it. But you can analyse too much. You can analyse all you like. People have problems and that's all there is to it. The fact is, whether we like it or not, there are no single, identifiable reasons for love coming to an end. All that happens is that one day it just stops. You wake up one morning and you say to yourself:

—Where's it gone? I wonder, where could our love have gone?

I didn't say it because for me it never happened. I never woke up thinking that in my life. I know Catherine did – but not me. It might have been better, perhaps, if I had. But that simply wasn't the way things had happened.

I'd literally spend hours daydreaming about them. Daydreaming about them and the lovely life they lived. I could see Ivan and Catherine on holiday, sitting in the lounge bar in the cool of a Greek summer evening. Sipping cocktails and listening to the music – just a piano player going through standards. Not John Martyn or anything like that.

'Cavatina', maybe, or 'Unchained Melody'. Ivan's hand would move across the table quite slowly – before reaching hers and touching it ever so gently. The French windows would be thrown open and you'd be able to feel the salt breeze on your face.

—This is a long way from Dublin, you'd hear him saying, it's a long way from Dublin and Ballyroan Road, Rathfarnham.

—It certainly is, my darling, she'd reply.

It was an idyllic scene and was the one which – against my better judgement – impelled me, irrationally, to decide to go out to their house one evening, completely on the spur of the moment. Immediately I arrived I knew something was wrong. The garden gate was chained, which it never was, and the house was enfolded in a desolate quiet. Their estate car was nowhere to be seen. I thought that perhaps they had actually moved house, or perhaps even had left the country altogether. My head was reeling as I stood there, quietly devastated on that leafy suburban road. It was as though I was standing on the top of Slievenageeha Mountain, and Imogen was waving to me from far away, her voice growing fainter all the time.

—Don't leave me, Immy! I cried, helplessly, plunging my face into my hands.

When I got back to the hostel, I became preoccupied again with thoughts of the photo. The hostel was silent, apart from the strange noises that often trouble an empty building. I couldn't settle – I kept walking around, searching

here, there and everywhere. Then it began to dawn on me –
the unthinkable had happened. The utterly unthinkable.
The photograph was gone!

I was perplexed. It became so bad I was actually *moaning*!
But then, almost instantaneously, I found myself swept up
by a wave of the most intoxicating pleasure, when I
discovered in its place an even *more* beautiful and tantalising
image – the most delectable portrait of Catherine Courtney!

Or, should I say, what *could* have been a delectable
portrait of my ex-wife. If she hadn't been in the company
of her Maltese lover, as they gazed so rapturously into one
another's eyes.

They were obviously having a real good time. It must
have been 110 degrees out there, on the illicit weekend
they'd shared in Malta. In Valletta, the capital, when
Catherine had told me she was going to be in Cork, visiting
her 'terribly ill' mother in hospital.

The most unacceptable aspect of the humiliating court
procedure was being told how and when I might see my
child. Pieces of time being fed to me like crumbs. I would
rather never have seen her at all than accept those terms. I
mean, your blood is your blood, as they used to say in
Slievenageeha. In the long run, it's thicker than anything.
And Immy was my blood-kin. That was my nature – she
was my heartbeat. And I couldn't have changed that even if
I'd tried. I'd finally accepted it that night in Bournemouth.

And once that has happened, there is no going back. I
appealed for strength and felt a powerful influence surging
through me.

—You won't be on your own – you can rely on me to shield you from wind and weather, Redmond. I'll always be there – till the very last pea is out of the pot, till the angels quit heaven's golden halls. Be assured of that.

My first intention had been to call to the house in Ballyroan Road, as soon as I knew for sure that Immy was on her own. With a story for her to the effect that I'd arrived over from London on a surprise visit and that her mother and Ivan were waiting – at this very moment! – in a hotel we'd secretly chosen in Killiney Village. A sort of impromptu get-together, I'd intended to say. The more I thought about that approach, though, the less sure I felt that she'd be convinced. Catherine would probably, over-protectively, have instilled in her all sorts of latent anxieties. In the end I decided to dispense with that altogether and instead concentrate on the 'final meeting with daddy' scenario. I was going away to America for good, I'd tell her, and had just wanted to see her one last time. I went to the doctor and got some more sleeping pills. I was happier than I'd been in a long long time as I crushed some capsules into a saucer that day, whistling along Drumcondra Road with my couple of bottles of Ribena.

—Ha, 'The Secret of Ribena!' I laughed, kind of giddily.

I had established over a period of time that Ivan and Catherine did their week's shopping in Dundrum every Sunday afternoon. Imogen rarely accompanied them on these trips – why I didn't know but was soon to find out. It was as if everything was falling perfectly into place.

83

At every turn I was being ably, if slyly and subtly, assisted, it seemed. For example, when I was going through the RTE Guide what did I discover? Only that on Sunday afternoons, RTE were showing reruns of *My Little Pony*! I was really startled when I came across that. But, of course, at the same time, it was lovely to know about it, for it made me feel confident that everything had been ordained to run smoothly and without incident.

And that soon we'd be arriving at our own special place, which up to now had existed only in the mind and in the memory of a chiming, bright, revolving carousel.

I knew in my heart that my precious angel would recognise me straight away, and that she'd probably be lost for words as soon as she saw what I'd brought as a present: *Where the Wild Things Are*, of course. Which did indeed prove to be the case. She started jumping up and down, to the extent that I actually had to take pains to calm her, sharing a few of our private little stories. Then I explained to her how I was going to America for 'quite a while', that I'd been given a job on the *New York Times* and was only back in Dublin for 'one special reason'. More than anything I wanted to get away from the estate but I couldn't afford to appear agitated. It was at that point I saw it, when she looked at me and smiled, and I knew then for sure that the hand of heaven was aiding and abetting me. There could be no mistaking the light that came into her eyes – almost imperceptible as it was. But there could be no mistaking that it had been there. I shivered in a private moment of acknowledgment and gratitude.

—I'll get my bag, I heard her say, but only for a little while for mammy might give out – OK?

I couldn't believe I was holding my daughter's hand. My heart beat with pride as she rested her head upon my shoulder.

All I wanted was to ease anonymously out of Ballyroan Road and then get properly into our stories, maybe even Zippy out of *Rainbow* would get a mention. We were bound for winterwood, obviously – but I wasn't in a position to tell her that yet.

Not, at least, until she'd had her Ribena.

I had saved up to buy the car. Not that it cost much, a few hundred is all. Although, even for that money, I could have tried to get myself a better model than an Escort for it cut out not once but fucking twice on the motorway.

For which reason, our journey to winterwood, you'd have to say, was both good and bad. Good and bad in equal measure. But, to be honest, mostly good, at least once we managed to get over our difficulties. Some aspects of which unsettle me even yet. For it turned out that she hadn't been watching *My Little Pony* at all – that was just for babies, she told me. What she'd, in fact, been watching was something called *Sweet Valley High*. I knew nothing about that and it made me feel depressingly inadequate. Which resulted in my becoming, I have to say, somewhat agitated. Requesting her, far earlier than I'd anticipated, to open the bottle and consume its contents.

—Drink the Ribena, pet! I said drink the Ribena! just as

I turned off the M50 intersection, not far from the pines and Rohan's Confectionery.

To tell you the truth, I would have given anything if both parts, of the journey I mean, could have been *equally* good. But I'm sufficiently objective enough to know that at no point was that ever likely to happen. Sooner or later, I knew, some small thing was going to go wrong. Maybe if hadn't been so preoccupied with thinking about Ned, and the more conciliatory attitude I'd been adopting towards him of late. To the extent, even, of almost forgetting what had happened between the two of us that terrible night. Which I know must sound strange. But there was something in me that kept persisting that we really ought to try and see the good inside people. Try to understand what it is that makes them act in the way they do.

And the more I thought like that, the more I felt that I had to accept that poor old Ned – he'd seen his share of suffering too.

A simple glance at the papers could tell you that.

Certainly in the tabloids he had been treated excessively harshly. Heartlessly tried and summarily convicted, really. It was hard, if you were in any way reasonable, not to reflect on how difficult it must have been for him – to be portrayed as though he were some kind of demon. His resentment, then, I would find myself thinking, being justified, really, if only to some small degree. I could feel myself gradually beginning to understand why he might feel the need to 'return', as it were. In order that his spirit might at last find some kind of ease. To use the opportunity, maybe, to give his side of the story. Simply to state his case.

I mean, there could be no doubt about it. There was no way on earth anyone could argue that he had been given a fair trial. He had been hounded from pillar to post by journalists and clergy (who didn't have an awful lot to be proud of themselves, in that regard, and whose self-righteousness, really, beggared belief) long before the case had even come to court.

Then, when it did, it being a complete waste of time. For no one had been prepared to listen to him for a second. And I knew what feelings like that could be like. For my story too had been dismissed out of hand, when Catherine and I were in court, I mean. It was hard, obviously, for jury members and the ordinary readers of newspapers to accept that an elderly man's friendship with a little boy – especially someone as sweet and innocent-looking as Michael Gallagher – had become so intense as to take him over completely. But there was plenty of evidence to suggest that that was indeed what had happened.

Pretty much, in fact, as it had in my own case. As regards my friendship with Imogen, I mean. Except that in our case you obviously couldn't call it 'friendship'. You could only call it love, the bond that existed between my daughter Immy and I. And if that's idealisation – well then, so be it.

I'm sorry, Catherine, but I can't help it, I found myself thinking, you shouldn't have given me an angel from heaven. Whom I love so much, with a love of the purest and rarest kind.

But the more I kept thinking about it, the clearer it became that everything was slowly but surely beginning to right itself. I found myself consumed by a new sense of purpose. And I also found myself hoping that by the simple fact of extending some humanity towards poor old Ned, offering the unfortunate wretch some small degree of genuine understanding, that I myself had played some worthwhile role in this new and most welcome world of equanimity. Some small part, however insignificant.

Maybe in his own way, that was all Ned had been looking for that unfortunate night in the hostel. Maybe that was the reason he had manifested himself to me and me alone. Hoping that I – I guess as an old friend – would be prepared to say:

—Yes, I understand, Ned. I genuinely do. I've been listening intently and finally I understand. I know you're not a bad man. I know it because, Ned, I've been there. I've been through the mill as well.

Deep down inside, the more I thought about it the more I became convinced that that was indeed what he'd wanted. *Needed*, in fact. But this at the time I'd been too emotionally vulnerable myself to understand. I hadn't, to be frank, understood the man at all. But now I did. I had lent him the sympathetic ear he needed, and that was all the man required. As soon as that consideration occurred to me, an all-engulfing wave of optimism swept over me as the Escort shot past yet another housing estate.

I had this feeling that everything was coming good. Righting itself bit by bit.

—Thanks, I heard Ned whisper – his voice as clear as day now – and I found myself grinning from ear to ear.

It was kind of beautiful, in a way. The world now seemed utterly transformed and I was so enraptured by developments that I didn't speak for ten whole minutes. Then I said:

—Are you all right in the back there, Immy?

I could see she was. The Ribena at last had begun to work.

—Thank heaven for that, I said, a little edgily. My daughter smiled sleepily and her little arm flopped down.

I sighed and drummed out a little tune on the wheel – the theme tune from *Rainbow*, as a matter of fact. My eyes were shining in the mirror, my copper-red curls hanging down over my forehead. It was hard to believe, I said to myself, that it all should work out like this. It was also strange thinking that I wouldn't be seeing Ned again. Now that his spirit, at long last, was at rest. Now he no longer had anything to worry him. Now that, at last, he'd been finally *understood*. I considered it a small and private personal triumph, and vowed to share it with Catherine when I eventually saw her.

As I somehow knew in my heart I was going to.

It had taken me quite by surprise on that winterwood journey the sheer volume of what Imogen remembered, babbling away as her eyelids, at last, began to droop. For instance, as soon as I mentioned Zippy out of *Rainbow*, her big eyes shone with this magic glow of recognition. I could see how much she valued it – just being able to have these conversations again.

—*Sweet Valley High*, I said, that's a load of rubbish. We

can't be bothered with that, can we, Immy? It's Zippy and Bungle we want, like old times.

It was like no time had passed since Kilburn at all. As we drove by the grim-looking industrial parks, making our way to our winterwood home, I laughed when I thought of her bringing up the 'afraid' things after she'd taken her first drop of Ribena.

—Here we come, Kimono! I remember laughing. Kimono, darling, and Pinkie Pie! Magic Castle, here we come!

Mid-Nineties

Four: Snakes Crawl at Night

Bɪʟʟ ᴄʟɪɴᴛᴏɴ ᴀʀʀɪᴠᴇᴅ ɪɴ Ireland to help sort out the problems in Ulster. I saw him on the television but didn't take much notice. Don't bother with politics at all these days. Hard as it might be to believe, I'm still too busy thinking about the man I once knew as Ned Strange – succumbing, as I so often do, to a certain nagging regret that I didn't listen more carefully to his stories when I had the chance. But also, far more importantly, attending to the advice and wisdom which he'd – as I realise now – been doing his best to pass on to me. It's still hard not to see him sitting there, astride the rocking chair, the stogie lolling lazily between his lips, saying:

—There's not much changes in this life, the way I see it. Things now is the same as a thousand year ago. My woman left me as many's a woman has done on her man. She strayed from the conjugal bower, Redmond, and I tell you, partner, I was drunk for a week. One whole week I tumbled about this valley and I didn't even know my name. I wouldn't have known my name if you'd asked me. I daresay I'm not the first and I know I'll not be the last. The way it is – you're given a glimpse of the heart's enchantment and just as you're getting to like it, you look up one day and there it's gone, for ever, burnt up like ashes. Not too many has answers about things like that – how to stop it happenin' or to make the pain go away. High up or low down, regal prince or low-bred mongrel, that's a puzzler as has got no solution. That's what you call the human condition, Redmond, the never-ending quiz show of what happens between a man and a woman.

It's hard for me to forgive myself now, for not having credited him with a little more intelligence. Now that a lot of time has passed, and a lot of water has indeed flowed under the bridge, I'm able to see just how completely and utterly misguided I was – if not, more accurately, just how plain *wrong*.

Maybe if I had exhibited a little more empathy then, and shown a little more respect for his experience, instead of patronisingly excavating it and turning it into what amounted, really, to journalistic whimsy, the poor man's life mightn't have ended the way it did. Hanging cold and alone in a prison shower cubicle.

It truly was a deeply depressing thought.

But that doesn't, and never will, take away from the fact that, in our time, the pair of us had enjoyed some terrific conversations. A substantial proportion of which I'll treasure for ever. And I know that he had liked some of my articles too. He told me. In particular, 'Children's

Games in Old God's Time', which I'd illustrated with a few drawings of my own. Which he considered 'truly excellent', I was told.

—Then, of course, your Uncle Florian was a dab hand at the drawing, as I recall, a bit of a maestro – when he wasn't dancing hornpipes, isn't that right? When he wasn't being The Twinkletoe Kid!

He could be strikingly articulate, Ned, when he wanted. Extremely sophisticated in his own way. But I seemed to find it difficult to bring myself to acknowledge that. As though I was the only mountain native privileged enough to be considered 'intelligent'. Certainly he was more so than some ordinary old hillbilly who'd never left the valley in his life. Another story he told me that I have to say was quite charming was the one about the day he planted the rose with Annamarie.

—That flower was for her, he said, the first rose of summer that would bloom for Annamarie Gordon.

He lifted down the fiddle and began to play a Tom Moore melody. Its soft lilting arpeggios lightly skimmed the kitchen's walls.

—That would have been about the third or fourth time we went out walking together. Would you like to know what kind of dress she was wearing? A blue one it was, a lovely blue dress with a clasp in her hair. It was cornflower blue and it looked real good on account of it matching the dress. She looked like an angel dropped down from heaven so she did. I worshipped the ground she walked upon, Redmond. I'd give my life to have her back. I'd give my whole life for one more day with Annamarie, to be sitting here with her, my life's partner – as we, at that time, swore we would always be.

It was sad to think of the two of them sitting there, conversing like that – telling one another, presumably, about the depth of their love. The depth of it, of course, and the inevitability of its endurance. Which is all you can think of when your heart is enchanted, when you're lying in the garden where you know roses will always grow, as far away from the black, void waste as can possibly be imagined.

Where the word 'outlands' has never existed.

One thing that cheers me, whenever I find myself looking back on it – and which I can take some pride in, I suppose – is the fact that I never forgot to bring him his cassette tapes, and that never failed to bring a smile to his face. Not to mention stimulating conversation, especially after a few copious mugs of you-know-what.

He had an old Sanyo cassette recorder held together with twine and you could hear it playing from morning till night, one country and western tune following another. Tales of love affairs and deaths and disasters. There wasn't one of those songs he didn't know, as if each one represented a chapter from his life. He often insisted he'd been 'marked' in some way. From way back, he said.

—It all started the day mama died. She got killed, you see, Redmond.

—I didn't know your mother was in an accident, I replied, dutifully.

—Two hundred and fifty bones bruk! he continued

wildly. They say it was one of the worst smashes ever seen on the mountain. That's no lie I'm telling you now, Redmond. Because if you go up to the ravine where it happened, you'll see the rocks below are like razors. And that's where the poor unfortunate woman landed. Ah yes, life be's sad, there's no doubt about it. That's why I like these auld country boyos. Ned, they'll say, why are you always listening to them old-time tunes? All we can hear is keening and yowling. Not true, I say to them, Redmond, and you'll see this when you get a bit older – them tunes isn't telling any lies! If there's one thing them songs is peddling it's the truth. They're just painting them in colours that suits what it is they're saying. When my mother was in that wreck, Redmond, I didn't feel just like crying a bit. Oh, no. I cried enough to fill seven seas. Them hurts is big, son. Just like the songs say. They ain't telling no lies at all. It's just that in the old times you'd readily admit that your heart was bruk, and have no problem saying you found it hard to go on. Nowadays they's so busy keeping going that whenever they stop it'll hit twice as hard. But that's not my problem, Redmond. These modern folks – what they'll have to do is find new songs of their own. I'm staying put with my old country lilters. Them's the boys can see inside my head, although I have to admit that most times it's all a-tangle. Has been, in fact, since the day I first got born. Or, like I say, even before. He winked and snorted gruffly.

—When my daddy fucked mama on that old feather bed!

You could see his teeth flashing as he trawled for my reaction.

—That's what I often used to think, Redmond. That maybe he raped Mama. Maybe Daddy went and raped old Mama. Maybe that's how Ned's got this feeling he's been marked.

Then he said:

—*Haw haw!* Sure I'm only kidding, Redmond. *Rape be damned!* My darling mammy never got raped. My loving daddy wasn't that kind of a man. He had better things to do than go around assaulting his own wife. Sure the auld bitch'd have given him her old pussy any time. *Haw haw*, Redmond! Any time he wanted – any time his tallywhacker wanted pleasure, my sweet mama would willingly part her two fat pins. No, Redmond, my mam and pap they was decent people. Sure they was! Wasn't they mountaineers? But it just goes to show, it's hard to trust anybody. You wouldn't know who is trying to sucker you and who isn't. I mean – for all I know you might be trying to sucker me. Mightn't you, Redmond? I might think I'm doing it to you – but maybe it's me's being codded all along. Maybe you're stealing *my* stories for *your* own purposes? Couldn't it be? Sure it could! You wouldn't know who to trust on this mountain – we're renowned for that, aren't we, us country folks? And after all, you were reared right here, were you not? So it'd be in you. Mischief and double-dealing might just be in your blood too. Is it, Redmond? Are you at heart a manipulative twister? Tell me, Redmond, might you be – or *are* you – a *snake?*

—Of course I'm not! How can you say such a thing? How can you even *think* of saying it?

He looked at me and sniggered.

—That's a good answer, Redmond, he said. Why, I'd

almost even believe you! You're a good one, Redmond. A chip off the old block. If your father was here he'd be mighty proud of you. Dang sure he would. As sure as Adam he ate the apple. As sure as Adam he ate the fucking apple!

Sometimes, when he was sufficiently in his cups, he'd stumble across the floor and shove a Charley Pride tape into the machine. Charley sang 'Snakes Crawl at Night'. It was a tune that exerted a particular effect on Ned Strange. Once he grabbed his violin in a fury.

—I'll smash this fucking fiddle in bits! he snapped. Do you hear me, Redmond? Do you fucking hear me? Do you hear me, Redmond Hatch, you cunt?

On that particular occasion it was only with the greatest difficulty I succeeded in placating him. He threw his arms around me and began to weep. Then, out of nowhere, he started chuckling again. When I looked at him, his shoulders were rocking and I paled as I saw him grinning – literally from ear to ear.

—Of course the whole fucking lot could be a pack of lies, Redmond. Maybe I don't give a fuck about these stupid country songs. Maybe it's like my stories about America. Maybe I *didn't* ever set foot beyond the mountain. That's a real possibility, isn't it, Redmond? That I might never, in fact, have travelled an inch further than them fucking pines there standing outside. I might only have been as far as the town, never further. How do you know but there never was a sweetheart either? That Annamarie Gordon never even existed? Why, us rascally mountain mongrels, you couldn't trust our oath!

He elbowed me provocatively, badgering me, repeating:

—Isn't that right, Redmond? Isn't that right, my comrade, my loyal fellow traveller?

He straddled the chair and remained silent for a long time. Then he lit a stogie and closed one eye, resting his elbow on his knee as he fixed me unyieldingly, his manner altering quite dramatically again. He drew a long breath through tobacco-stained teeth.

—Imagine her doing the like of that, Redmond, sliding her pins apart in order to pleasure a cash-rich cunt! A little innocent creature the likes of Annamarie Gordon! Giving her body to a snake like Olson. It's hard to credit. Hard to credit, Redmond, son.

He told me they'd first met in the winter of 1963. It was one of the severest winters on record. The valley had been snowbound for over two weeks.

—That was the first time I felt like someone, Redmond, he went on to explain. Felt like saying to myself: 'Yes, Ned, you've done it. You're somebody at last. She's turned you into a fully grown man.' After meeting that lady I was the king of the mountain. From that moment on, she made me believe that I could become someone special. That her and me, we could change the world. She changed it all when she said: 'I love you.' 'I love you, Edmund Strange' – she said that to me, Redmond.

Regarding my own pronouncement upon that particular subject, I had first revealed my innermost feelings to

Catherine Courtney in a café in Cork City, in late summer 1980. I was eating a cheese omelette and she was having Black Forest gateau. I'd been building up to it for weeks.

—You have no idea how much I'm in love with you, I said.

—Oh Redmond, I remember her saying, as she put her hand, just wrapped it warmly and gently, around mine.

Ned had declared his feelings when they were walking together in the snow. He told me she had reciprocated fully.

—I just couldn't believe she'd uttered those words, he said.

They decided soon after that they would be married – and planned the ceremony for a couple of years hence. They agreed that when their little baby arrived they would treat it as if it was the only child ever to be born in the world. There was no end to the presents they were going to buy for it. No end to the songs they intended to sing to it. They spent hours by a flowing stream, staring at their blooming rose and thinking up new names. They must have thought up at least a thousand. If it happened to be a boy they were going to call it Owen because that had been Ned's father's name and Annamarie said that she thought that would be nice. Ned just couldn't contain himself, he told me.

—It was wonderful being there, just sitting by that babbling brook. It was a far cry from the outlands, that was for certain sure, he said.

As far as a human being could possibly get.

*   *   *

Then it happened, that night he left the pub. He'd been having a few drinks with some farmers from the valley but had decided, simply on a whim, to go home. His pals asked him why he was leaving and he'd simply responded: 'No reason at all.' It certainly wasn't because he was harbouring any suspicions with regard to his wife's behaviour. For he'd never have dreamt in a million years that Annamarie Gordon would indulge in anything so base and heart-burning as cheating. If you'd been forward enough to ask him why, that was what he'd have readily and honestly and confidently replied: 'Because it isn't in her.'

But that was where Ned was wrong. It *was* in her. A realisation which began to dawn on him, not so very long after he'd left the pub, when he found himself staring in amazement across the valley. As the headlights of a car – a limousine Cadillac – tore off down the mountain, his wife stood waving in its wake. That was John Olson's car, he mused quietly to himself.

A massive hand seemed to lift up the mountain.

When Ned arrived, he and his wife talked about nothing in particular. Then Ned said:

—I was wondering, Annamarie, whose was the car that was here just now?

Annamarie didn't answer. Maybe she hadn't heard him, Ned found himself thinking. So he thought he'd perhaps better say it again.

—Car, Annamarie replied, I'm afraid there was no car.

—No car, said Ned, well now, that's funny because the problem is there was. I seen it you see.

—Did you? said Annamarie.

—Yes I did, replied her husband.

Well, such a beating as Ned meted out to his wife that night. Talk about not lifting your hand to your wife. Why the poor woman was practically unrecognisable when he'd finished.

—Oh, yes! he'd laugh, slapping his cap against his knee as he continued his story. The women can be divils, Redmond! So you be careful – you hear me now, my young partner?

I shifted uneasily in the chair. His intensity showed no sign of abating.

—Yes, you be careful, Redmond. For the women'll say: What car? they'll say. Nope sorry seen no car, what man? I seen no man there was no man in here! There was no man's tallywhacker inside of me, Ned! That's what they'll say! And keep on saying it until there's damn all avenue open to you but—

A desperate cry escaped his lips.

—*I didn't mean to do it, Redmond!* I didn't mean to drown her, I didn't! Say you understand that, Redmond, my boy! She shouldn't have permitted his tallywhacker in! A long pause ensued. I couldn't believe my ears. He was sitting with his back to me but there could be no mistaking it – he was laughing again. I wanted to get the hell out. I felt cold all over.

—Oh, the women! I heard him chuckle. The women are divils because they leave you no choice! Get in there, Annamarie, get in like a good girl! Ha ha, you bitch – '*Glug glug*,' she says!

*   *   *

103

The night was drawing in and I longed to get home. All I wanted was to get back to Catherine. We'd been planning to go to Rudyard's that weekend. That was a restaurant she'd loved in what is now Temple Bar. Whenever we had the money we always made a point of going there.

When I came back to myself, Ned was standing above me, blubbering, with the tears pouring out of him like some heart-broken little baby. I consoled him as best I could, staring out the window, trying to think of nothing but the woman I loved. Trying my best not to hear Ned's heart-broken pleas, as they struggled to free themselves from his confused and bitter soul. A soul which, once again consumed by wicked mocking laughter, swept out into the night and the tall imprecating pines.

When Catherine's solicitor wrote to me and told me that, irrespective of my protestations, I had no rights whatsoever apart from those stipulated by the court of law, I wandered the streets of London, scooped-out and empty, steered towards the place where no roses grow, the exterior darkness where there is only stony ground. Where even the idea of a rose would seem farcical. I'd think of Ned and what he used to say:

—Them's the outland fields, Redmond. The most barren fields in the world. And I ought to know – for I wandered them long enough.

I sat in Queen's Park the best part of a day. You never know how special ordinariness is until you wake up one day and it's gone. Queen's Park was where me and Immy had invented winterwood. I remembered that day so vividly. We'd been having breakfast that morning and unexpectedly *The Snowman* came on. We continued eating our cornflakes, the pair of us mesmerised as we watched him walk on air, oblivious of all the little houses below.

—He lives in it, doesn't he? I remembered her saying. That's where he lives, in winterwood, Daddy.

—Oh, yes – perhaps he does! I said, not thinking.

—*Of course* he does, you silly man! she chided me. Him and the Snow Princess!

I laughed and nodded.

—Whatever you say, my dear, I said.

We'd sit there on that bench as she twisted her bobbin and sang songs to herself, adrift in a private world of her own. Then, all of a sudden, she'd point up and say:

—Look! He's walking in the air . . . !

I wouldn't be concentrating and she'd bristle whenever I'd say:

—Who? Who's that, Imogen?

—Oh, *you*! was all she'd say.

Because, of course, she'd have meant the Snowman.

For some reason as I walked those desolate London streets, more than anything I'd keep thinking about the day we had bought the coat. The woman in Harrods could see how excited we both were.

—It really suits her, she'd said as she fixed the collar, she's a picture. What's her name?

—Immy, I said, without thinking.

—*Imogen!* my daughter corrected, slapping me playfully with her mitten.

—Well, Imogen's a picture, the assistant insisted.

To show you just how much those days actually meant, once, when I happened to be passing a children's clothes shop on the Kilburn High Road, out of the corner of my eye I saw a coat the very same as Immy's. I'm not saying it was *exactly* the same – just similar. All I could think of was: I wonder what they're doing in Dublin right now? I would have caught a plane right there and then but it simply wasn't physically possible.

It was to be some time before I found myself in a position to do that. And there were a few things I had to think about first.

Before I – as Ned might have had it – combined with myself in 'bold conspiracy'.

To alter the path of my life before I was destroyed.

After they'd gone, every day, without fail, I went to that park. I read Maurice Sendak over and over. And thought about the old days. Not just with Immy but with my own parents as well. Before my mother died she used to come to my bedroom late at night and turn the night light way on down. Then, ever so softly, she'd start singing – 'Scarlet Ribbons', the song mama loved. She used to tie a little ribbon to the bars above my bed. Tie it in a little knot, she said, and it will keep you safe and free from danger.

—It stands for our love. Little Redmond and his mam. A

little red ribbon that signifies their love. I love you, Little Red – for you're the only thing that keeps me alive.

That was what my mother said after she sang. After she'd sung our song 'Scarlet Ribbons'.

There was a haberdashery near the flat in Kilburn. I bought some ribbon there. I kept it in my pocket and twined it around my fingers.

—'Scarlet Ribbons', I'd hum to myself, wandering the aimless outland streets.

I even brought it home to Ireland, associating it, subconsciously, I suppose, with winterwood.

—You make up stories, I heard Ned whisper, you make up stories the very same as me. I know that because I know about your mother. She didn't die in a church. She died of a brain haemorrhage brought on by your father's beatings. That's how she died, you auld lying trickster!

—Shut up! Shut up, do you hear me? I'd snap – against my better judgement. But he knew how to get to me.

Then I'd see him laughing – his shoulders rocking as he teased his beard.

—The mountain and the pines will always be with you, Redmond. Always make sure you remember that. Always and everywhere you'll bring them with you.

How right he'd been. Every single place I went.

As a matter of fact, back in 1981, long before the truth about Ned's nature had emerged, I had actually been giving serious consideration to bringing Catherine home to Slievenageeha, around the time my first folklore articles had

107

begun to appear in the *Leinster News*. Articles which increased Ned's popularity quite considerably, I have to say.

—I don't know how to thank you, Redmond, he said. You're like a son to me now after all you've done.

Every Sunday the kiddies arrived at the schoolhouse for the ceilidh. They came from all over. Its growing popularity was truly astounding. But I had taken pains to emphasise its down-home, neighbourly aspect.

—The Slievenageeha Children's Ceilidh is about nothing so much as good neighbourliness. A happy community kicking up its heels and having itself a whale of a time.

For far too long, ceilidhs, I contended, had been seen as the preserve of a few worthy zealots intent on preserving 'authentic' Irish culture. Restricted to a couple of earnest convent girls dancing a hornpipe in a draughty school hall, stiff as boards with their arms by their sides.

—That day is gone, I wrote. A new day dawns for Irish ceilidh. Now it's all about exuberance, good humour and excitement. And it is all happening at Slievenageeha school-house every Sunday at 3 p.m.

The great thing about Ned – apart from, of course, being a wizard with the bow – was that he was a terrific music teacher. And, it goes without saying, a wonderful communicator.

—And he's just so solid and dependable, everyone said. It's like he's your father or something. It's like you could trust him with just about anything, really.

'Ned of the Hill', I called him in my articles. He thought it was the 'bee's knees', he told me. Slapping his thighs, chuffed as he guffawed:

—Ned of the Hill! Well, I have to hand it to you, Redmond, you're a good one! As a result he started to sing it at the ceilidhs, the famous old ballad of the same name. Sawing away as he stuck out his chest, the kids singing along (he'd taught them all the words) as his strong, proud voice rang out across the valley:

Adeir Eamonn a' Chnoic: a lao ghil's a chuid
Cad do dheanfainn-se dhuit?
Mara gcuirfinn ort beinn dom ghuna?

Which meant, as he explained:

Says Ned of the Hill: my love fond and true
What else could I do?
But shield you from wind and weather?

One day, over a glass of clear, he looked up at me and grinned as he said:

—There's good words, ain't they, Redmond?

—Yes, I wholeheartedly agreed, really lovely lyrics, Ned. I like them.

—You do, do you? They're very like one I was singing that first day. The very first day you arrived in Slievenageeha. Do you remember that one, Redmond? It was about hell, Redmond. Hell. Do you know how long it says you might expect to dwell in such a place? Do you know how long, Redmond, as a matter of fact? You don't, well I'll tell you.

He pinched his nose and roared phlegm into the grate, before launching into his 'high lonesome' song:

109

Here we both lie in the shade of the trees
My partner for ever just him and me
How long will we lie here O Lord who can tell?
Till the winter snow whitens the high hills of hell.

He shivered ominously. Then he looked at me again and said:

—That's how long, Redmond. That's how long you and me can expect.

I must have dozed off and when I came to, I called his name but he was nowhere to be seen. The door was wide open as the wind came blowing in from the mountain. He didn't arrive back until the following morning. I had no idea where he'd been and he didn't offer any explanation.

Acting as if nothing at all had happened.

The Innocent: A Nation Mourns
The Lonely Death of Michael Gallagher

What the papers had reported, no one could have imagined, not in their worst nightmares.

The *Independent* photograph, particularly, painted the ghastliest of melancholic scenes, a dismal shot of blacks and slate-greys, with the blurred pines beyond the factory possessing a deeply sinister aspect.

Whenever I read about it, deeply familiar but unwelcome feelings would return once more to torment me and I'd see him standing there, looking out of the dark.

—Something dreadful is going to happen, Redmond, and when it does, believe me – you'll know!

I eventually came to see, however, by simply *concentrating*, just how absurd it had all been.

The man was dead, for heaven's sake – hadn't he hung himself?

In a prison shower of all places. The evidence was there in black and white. Of course it was. It was hard not to laugh. In the end I became embarrassed, actually, that I had ever given it any credence. He hadn't even been *there*. In the bed or in the landing or anywhere else. Such are the unfortunate by-products of emotional trouble, I told myself. It got to the stage in the end where I had almost *completely* forgotten the whole ridiculous episode.

I was a new man, truly, and it really was wonderful. I hadn't undergone anything like the old stress in months. So that, I remember thinking, I probably wouldn't have been able to describe such a condition if I'd been asked to. I was moving closer to a state of complete contentment. Very at ease with myself indeed.

Which was the way, I knew, things were destined to stay. Those were the thoughts which were going through my head as Immy and I drove onwards towards winterwood. When I pulled up at some lights, it seemed like I'd been waiting for ages for them to change. And it was at that point I smelt it, the heart-sinking sodden *dampness*. You hear of people saying the blood just 'drained from his face'. But you rarely, if ever, witness it happen. I caught a glimpse of my face in the mirror and I'm not exaggerating when I baldly state it was the colour of death.

I didn't have to turn. I knew he was there. His leering eyes staring from the window where he was parked. He looked like he'd been drinking for days. Suddenly he shot forward as the lights turned to green.

—Soon, Redmond, *soon*, I heard him say.

I know I ought never to have stopped in Blanchardstown – it almost ruined things. But I couldn't stop thinking about *Sweet Valley High*, which Imogen had been watching instead of *Pony*. It unsettled me so much because I hadn't been expecting it. Which was why I reacted as soon as I saw the restaurant, rising up out of nowhere, just appearing through the haze of rain: Deep Pan Pizza.

—Who's for salami and who's for pineapple? I could hear Catherine crying.

Slumped in the back seat, poor Imogen was moaning. She'd been asking me for something, but what with all that happening I couldn't focus on what it was. I think she was saying her mouth was dry – and it upset me. But I never intended to shout at her. There is only one reason why I spoke harshly to Immy, and three words explain it – Piper fucking Alpha. He was the reason I snapped at my daughter:

—Shut up, Immy! Do you hear me now!

It had happened as soon as I returned to the car. It was stress, that was all. The only other time in my life I had ever spoken to my daughter like that was the time she had spilt the paint over herself, in Kilburn. She had been playing

112

with some poster paints and went and got her clothes covered in them. Things hadn't been going well that week, either, you see. I'd had three articles turned down one after another and Catherine had been giving me a very rough time. But that didn't matter now, I told myself. Not now that we were almost there.

That was all I kept thinking as I drove – if only I hadn't met Piper Alpha the fool. If only I hadn't been unfortunate enough to meet him in Deep Pan Pizza. If only that hadn't happened, I kept repeating, as we carried onwards to our winterwood home.

Late Nineties

Five: Redmond Place

THE EVENTS OF THAT summer, tense as they were, if not terrifying, even, they all seem so distant now. Part of the faded fabric of history, I suppose, and generally I tend not to think too much about them. A summer long past, yet another skin shed. Such were my feelings throughout the latter part of the prosperous nineties. Bill Clinton was still in the White House, and the North of Ireland had settled into a relative calm. It looked like we were entering into a whole new phase of optimism. I certainly was. Things had turned out spectacularly well. An extramural course I attended in DCU – my first real *public* outing as Dominic Tiernan, secured with the aid of impeccably forged references from the now defunct *North London Chronicle* amongst others – provided me with a very promising opportunity: a possible placing with a newspaper. A Dublin weekly which would soon be established, I was informed.

To make a long story short, I was successful in my application. Obviously I had to be careful and more than a little economical with the truth. I was extremely nervous, I might as well be honest. But what with my leather jacket, long hair and ponytail, which I had dyed, I looked nothing now like the old Redmond Hatch, more like Willie Nelson, perhaps, or a New Age hippy-style executive. And, gradually, any worries I had in that respect began to recede.

Anyway, as I say, I secured the position, at a generous salary commensurate with the prosperous times, which was wonderful. They even treated me to a meal to celebrate, as a result of which I found myself totally unprepared for what was about to happen later that evening, in the new apartment which I'd just moved into, in Herbert Park on the south side of Dublin. The moment I turned the key in the door I felt something was amiss – then I saw them: just a few random pieces of silver tinfoil lying there. Then – in literally a matter of seconds after I'd registered them – the depressingly familiar, unpleasant, sodden dampness. It seemed to fill the entire space. Then it came – I stiffened from head to toe. The voice was low but clear and audible.

—Olson gave her *The Heart's Enchantment*. Did the Maltese cunt give your whore any books?

It was coming from the direction of the potted plants beneath the window.

It hurt me so much, hearing Catherine Courtney described like that. It made me resentful and angry and bitter. And now, more than ever, I wanted him to know. The time had come for me to act at last. I had been cowed and compliant for far too long. Now, finally, it would have to be made clear to Ned Strange that these insane provocations could no longer be indulged. I clenched my fists and steeled myself to confront him. I could just make out his shadow behind the potted plants. His name rose to my lips but then I heard him pleading helplessly, up to his old schemes and manipulative tricks:

—You don't really believe that I would hurt a little boy, do you, Redmond?

I snapped – I couldn't help it.

—But you did, I cried. That is exactly what you did!

Suddenly I smelt the most extraordinary aroma of roses. And looked up to see a businesswoman in a smart two-piece suit staring at me, spraying some perfume on to her wrist as she tucked her briefcase under her arm.

—I think the weather is about to improve, she said, coughing politely as she pressed the security button.

Troubling as that incident admittedly was, in retrospect I'm glad it happened. Because it pulled me up short, made me realise I would have to take myself in hand. And stop prevaricating where Ned Strange was concerned. If I didn't I would only have myself to blame.

And I did, I'm glad to be able to say.

Because the simple facts were, and I could see them clearly now, that any sympathy for the likes of Strange were always going to be a complete waste of time. All along I'd been deceiving myself, appealing like a fool to a good-natured side that simply didn't exist. The facts were there. There was only one way they could be interpreted. And the more I examined those, with the aid of my assembled cuttings and newspaper reports, the more I experienced a sense of gratification, as I sat there one evening in the corner of a dimly lit pub in Ballsbridge.

And not only that, but gratitude too. Gratitude that justice in the case had indeed been done. That Ned Strange had indeed met the end he deserved. A shudder of *schadenfreude* went rippling through me and it had the most uplifting effect. I was delighted, actually, the more I went through the facts, spreading the reports on the table as I sat there. Overjoyed that he'd been tried, found guilty and sentenced to life. But that wasn't all I was pleased about – I had no problem at all admitting I was glad he'd done himself in, the least punishment he could expect to face after the heinous crimes the old fucker had committed. Which were an affront to humanity, nothing more and nothing less. May hell roast him, I found myself thinking, as I ordered another drink. Something which I think I'd have been afraid to do before. But not now. No fucking way – not now.

—You'll never be free, Strange, I spat bitterly as I downed my double whiskey, you'll be lying there in that lonely cold grave till the mountains crumble and the pines rot away. Till your so-called snow whitens your lonesome high hills! You hear that, Ned? That's how long you'll be in there waiting – and, boy, do you deserve it, my friend! Nobody deserves it more than Ned Strange!

I'd read that his coffin had been returned to Slievenageeha, to be buried in the cemetery near his home, the old familiar tumbledown cabin where he'd toyed with me, amusing himself for want of something better to do. But not any longer. Not any longer, Mr Ned Strange. Ha ha, I had to laugh. When I thought of how timid I had been in the past, afraid to contradict him, hopelessly, meekly, looking away. Ned fucking Strange, I thought.

What on earth could I possibly have been afraid of?

I sipped the alcohol as relief swept through me. Not surprisingly, I suppose, because after all, I now could accept, it was plainly evident that in his case justice had, in the end, been done. Justice which consisted of banishment to the outlands for all of eternity. No amount of trickery would ever succeed in getting him out of that. No amount of wiles or cleverly diverting 'yarns'.

The simple fact was, now, whenever the name of Ned Strange came up – whenever you thought of that shoulder-rolling figure in his old plaid shirt and battered corduroy britches, whenever you thought of that old-time mountain man – there was only one word which would rise to your lips. And it wouldn't be 'Ned of the Hill' or 'good old Ned' either. No. There was only one name he would go by now:

Ned Strange, the conniving, black-hearted *paedophile*.

All the same, there can be no denying that human beings tend to be unpredictable. For, shaken as I was after all my deliberations, it was hard not to be just the smallest bit moved by what I happened to come across in Palmerston Park on my way back from lunch the following afternoon. Reminding me as it did of me and Ned on one of our more amenable days on the mountain, long before the appalling truth had emerged. I couldn't believe it when I saw it lying there, with its two legs stiff on a small bed of leaves. It was inevitable, I suppose, that it would remind me of him, of that special afternoon when he had erupted into a truly lyrical rendition of a song. It was winter and it was the snow which had prompted it – it being, as I recall, the first fall of the year. He'd gripped me by the arm and gasped excitedly:

—I want to sing you this little ditty, Redmond. It's a tune by Hank Williams. It's all about a little birdie that dies.

He'd sung it quite magnificently – let there be no doubt about that. Cradling the fiddle upon his shoulder and stroking the strings with the bow with such gentleness that the notes fell like the clearest drops of water, and he slipped off into a dream world, swaying from side to side, as the instrument, in a deep rushing undertone, mimicked the wind.

—'Did you ever see a robin weep, / When leaves began to die?'

In the light of such poignant memories, it was quite a precious moment, coming quite by chance upon it, that poor little robin. And, as I stood there looking at it, it really would have been difficult not to interpret it as a sign of some kind. A firm indication that our story was finally over – the story, I mean, of Edmund Strange and Redmond Hatch. He was in his grave now, in his Slievenageeha mountain home, and that was where he was going to stay. Being left with no choice but to accept now, finally, the grim sentence which had been pronounced upon him –

total unrest for all eternity. Interred alone in the barren outland fields. Where even the thought of a rose growing was laughable.

Somehow, as I stroked the robin's little domed head, I had this feeling that – this time for certain – Ned had, however reluctantly, accepted the situation and given in. At long last, capitulated. Accepted, after all this time, that his sentence – regardless of the behaviour of journalists, or anyone else for that matter – hadn't been in any way unjustified. That what he'd received he'd amply deserved. As though he were, at long last, confessing:

—His pathetic little cries! I had no right to harm Michael!

That, thankfully, was the tune he was playing now. You could sort of feel it permeating the placid air. I said a prayer in thanks to the poor little robin. Just like Imogen and I had done that day.

Because me and my Immy, we'd found one too.

Catherine had only just started working in Victoria Wine at the time, a mere stone's throw from Queen's Park station. I'm not pretending it was much of a job – to tell the truth they paid an absolute pittance. But it made us as proud as if she'd been crowned the Queen of England. I'll never forget the size of Imogen's small hand. There were leaves blowing around, lovely autumn leaves, just like there'd been in Palmerston Park. As though it were a premonition – as if somehow, instinctively, I could feel they were about to leave me – every so often I'd squeeze her hand tightly.

—Ow! she'd say. That hurt! and she'd lift her hand and gaze at it, affronted. Her little reddened fleshy hand.

—We're rich, I remember her saying, now Mummy's working.

Our cries of laughter pealed simultaneously. There was a great spreading beech in the middle of the park and it was just by the litter bin then that I saw it – a little robin redbreast, stiff as a board. With both its legs sticking up in the air. Imogen cried when I lifted it and stroked it. Out of nowhere a tear sprang to her eye.

—How did it die, Daddy? she said, but I couldn't speak. I just shook my head.

We buried it that evening in our garden. When the landlord heard what we had done he called to the door and demanded we dig it up. Apparently in our zealousness we had gone and disturbed some tenant's flowers. He said there were rules about that sort of thing. You might have expected us to have been hurt and angry – to have remonstrated, perhaps, and caused an unpleasant scene. But we didn't. We didn't even tell him we had buried a little robin. We were much too preoccupied for that. Preoccupied with our own happiness and well-being as a family. And we didn't share our private secrets. No one in winterwood ever did. So instead we just disinterred him and buried him the next day beside a tree in Queen's Park.

—I hope the mini-beasts don't get him, Dad, I remember her saying.

—They won't, I promised her.

We made him a cross, just the humblest little cross,

fashioned from rushes. I went over to Hackney marsh specially to get them. As a child I had seen my mother make one. There was a bitter wind blowing as we stood there that day with the autumn leaves all whirling around.

One on which – in happier times – you might have heard the voice of Ned Strange, before things had gone so dreadfully wrong. Singing his heart out, with the children all around him, some of them with their lower lips trembling pitifully as he told the story to all his 'little ceilidh partners', all about a little robin who had died alone.

Died alone, one day in the snow.

I remember him reading me a passage once, a piece from one of his tattered old westerns, pouring a mug of clear as we sat there by the fire, reading each sentence with an infinite, practised patience. The fire spread its enormous shadows on the ceiling, as he sipped from his jar and drew heavily on his stogie. Far off in the valley, a stray dog bark went sailing, dying somewhere miles beyond the mountain. There was a sepia photo of his father on the mantelpiece, standing in a field, wielding a scythe in an old plaid shirt. It made me unsettled – bearing, as it did, an uncanny resemblance to my own red-haired father. When I remarked on it to Ned, he just laughed and said:

—You're from the mountain, Redmond. What do you expect? And I'll tell you something else – deep down, you know, you're flawed the very same as me. What do you say, Red? Think you're like me – a liar and a deceiver? Are you a bit crafty, do you think? Leave out the bits that'll implicate and incriminate you?

125

—Shut up! I retorted sharply. I don't want to hear!

He laughed and then pretended it had all meant nothing.

—We're ordinary simple country folk, ain't we, Red? Mongrels, indeed! That's what they call us. Inbreds. Watchful and suspicious. Every one of them being married, they'll tell you, so much that they all end up being their own grandmothers.

His eyes flickered wilily.

—Grandmother. I'm not my own grandmother. We're not mongrels, are we, Redmond? Take you now. You're a sophisticated city boy. What with you working on a big paper and all.

He cracked his knuckles, before glaring at me as he spat. There could be no mistaking his antipathy now.

—Oh, yes, you're so fucking sophisticated – just like Olson! He was sophisticated too, the fucking snake!

I didn't want to hear any more of it. I wanted to go. Back to the city and my beloved Catherine Courtney. I was beginning to wonder now would I ever bother coming back near Slievenageeha? His taunts had begun irritating me most profoundly now, and my initial idea of compiling his 'mountain memories' into a book or biography of some sort had gradually, steadily, begun to lose its appeal. Sometimes he'd just sit there and say nothing at all, staring into the fire, lost in its deep vaults and chasms and winding galleries, dreaming of a girl in a simple blue dress. A simple blue dress with a matching hair clasp. Who'd planted a flower to symbolise their love.

—Don't talk to me of enchanted days. I want to hear

nothing of enchantment of the heart, he'd grind bitterly
through tobacco-stained teeth.

Once he asked me did I believe in God.

—Are you a believer, Redmond? he quizzed. You can tell
me.

I nodded. Then he started the old talk about hell. What I
thought about it. What it might be like. Before leaning
back on his chair and glaring, his knuckles paling as he
gripped the handle of a mug:

—Three blasts of an archangelic trumpet before your
soul's cast into the pit? That how you think of it, Redmond? A great clock ticking: 'Ever, never: ever, never.' Eh?
Or could it, maybe, be something even worse? The divil
himself lying by your side, shielding you, as the song says,
from wind and weather? Could it, maybe, be like that, do
you think? For ever!

I told him that I had to go, that Catherine would be
expecting me.

—Catherine, he muttered, with deep, biting sarcasm. It
won't last. Women, they change, and God help you when
they do. Everything they loved about you, why it turns
around now and makes them sick. The only one who really
loves you for always is your mother. And she's a goddess.
She's an angel. She's the only one who will never let you
down. Except your daddy had to go and kill yours, didn't
he? Beat her crooked like you might a helpless donkey. Give
her a haemorrhage so as you have to make up stories. Make
up stories about her dying in the chapel. Dying in the
chapel and singing the stupidest childish songs.

I didn't answer him. I said nothing, just sat there

smarting bitterly, bent double beneath the shadows. I stood up sharply. He pushed me back down.

—Stay awhile more I told you!

I joined him sullenly for one last drink.

He drew on the stogie and arched his right eyebrow.

—So then, Redmond – the two of us. You and me. Are we related, do you think?

I turned away, dismissively, from him.

—No way, I told him, we certainly are not.

He looked at me again and said:

—You sure about that?

—Of course I'm sure.

—You don't sound sure.

—I told you *I'm sure!*

—Red?

—What?

—We're *all* related! Every sonofabitch as was ever spawned on the slopes of this mountain! Don't you see that? Well, don't you, Red?

—I'm sorry, I said, I really must go.

—Red, you're not listening to me!

—I'm sorry. Like I said, I have to leave.

—Stay where you are, I said, Red! I mean *Ned!*

He took me by the shoulders and forced me, uncompromisingly, back into the chair. Then he stood there, smiling, rubbing his fist in a playful fashion. But there could be no mistaking the menace in his eyes. He towered above me, looking down without flinching.

—All I want you to tell me is – if you and me's not related – then how is your name Hatch?

—It's just my name. It just happens to be Hatch.

—It just happens to be! It just happens to be! Did you ever *happen*, as you say, did you ever happen to look up what it actually means? What 'hatch' happens to mean in the Irish language? You're not familiar with the Irish word *ait*? You do know how to pronounce that word, don't you, Redmond?

I did as a matter of fact. And was triumphant, at last, to be in a position to trump him.

—Yes, I replied cockily, it's pronounced 'atch'. It actually means 'place'.

He stood there and waited, stroking his chin as he pondered, biding his time with enviable control. Then slowly his grin began to widen, stretching right across his face.

—Sure it does, he said. It means that all right. But it also means something else, you see.

I could bear it no longer.

—What does it mean! I snapped. What does it fucking mean?

—Easy, he cooed.

He flashed his incisors. I went cold all over.

—It means 'strange', Little Redmond. That's what it means. It means 'strange'. I'm surprised at you not knowing that now. With you being an educated man and all.

I got up from my seat and tried to push past.

—Maybe you'll print that little nugget of information in your paper. Maybe you'll put that in your next article. I'm sure your readers would find it most interesting! Red Strange from the mountain – sounds kind of familiar, you have to admit.

When I got to the door I demanded bitterly:

—Tell me this. Be honest. Have you been making a fool of me all along?

—You mean, like when I told you my stories about Annamarie and all?

—Yes, I said, exactly.

—When I told you I drowned the lying bitch in the river?

—Yes, I said, and averted my eyes.

—Yes, Redmond, I'm afraid your suspicions all along have been right.

He paused and sighed as he looked out the window.

—It was all lies, Redmond. I didn't drown her.

When I heard those words, I calmed down immensely. To the extent that I actually admitted it, in fact.

—I'm so relieved to hear that, Ned, I said.

—Oh, are you? he said. You prefer what I did instead then, do you?

—What are you talking about?

He said nothing. I demanded straight out:

—What are you talking about? What are you saying?

He pushed me back and stood in the doorway, flicking his tongue against the back of his teeth.

—I knifed her, he said. Just like I did the other fucking bitch, Carla Benson, the so-called beauty of Boston. Redmond, you look pale. I think perhaps you need a drink. Why don't the two of us go right back inside?

I remembered the name Carla Benson well. Only months before he had described to me how he'd spent some months 'walking out' with her, as he'd put it, during the time he'd spent in Boston. It had troubled me so much that as soon as I got back to the city, I had gone straight to the National Library in Kildare Street and searched through the archives for issues of old American newspapers. Being similarly relieved when I succeeded in establishing that the names didn't correspond.

Except that when I broached it with him, he was ready again.

—Aye, but you see, her name wasn't Benson. Her name wasn't Carla Benson at all. I lied about that.

He leaned over to me when he said it, his two eyes like slits.

—Carla McIntyre – that was her name. Boys but I be's forgetful!

I literally ran from the cabin on that occasion. All the way down the mountain, I could have sworn I heard him laughing:

—Ned and Red! Together for ever! Till the winter snow whitens hell's highest hills!

I knew I shouldn't have gone back near the library – the first time had been ordeal enough. But as soon as I got back to Dublin, I went straight there and ordered the American papers from the archive again. I kept insisting to myself that the whole idea was quite preposterous, repeating what I'd been told a hundred times before. The same old refrain you heard in the mountain pub – the same one I'd heard that very first day:

—Pass no remarks on Ned. Sure you couldn't believe the old fool's oath, I'm telling you.

I would have given anything for that to be the case. But there it was before me in black and white letters. The officer in charge of the case was quoted as saying he'd never in his life seen anything like it.

—The poor woman was eviscerated. In fifty years' service I've never encountered such brutality.

As that which was inflicted on the unfortunate Carla McIntyre.

In the *Leinster News* office after that, they noticed that I'd become increasingly irritable. I couldn't for the life of me seem to shake her name off. I kept thinking of the officer and his description. Then I'd see Ned or *hear* him. Throwing back his head and saying:

—Boys O boys!

—You're like a bear with a sore head, my colleagues told me, lighten up.

Ultimately I knew I was faced with no choice – I would have to confront him. To that end I had rehearsed the scenario in my mind. It was as though he could anticipate the thoughts inside my head and I found that deeply intimidating.

I sat in his kitchen, stammering awkwardly as I repeated my accusations. I felt such a complete and utter fool. His whole body rocked with laughter.

—Boys O boys, but Redmond, I swear you're an awful man – where in heaven's name did you get such an idea? That I would go and do a thing the like of that? Sure I've never been out of the valley in my life – I haven't even been fortunate to have a girlfriend! Oh, sure, once upon a time there was a little sweetheart I had a dalliance with all right – a lovely little girl by the name of Annamarie Gordon, as I recall. And I have to admit I might have been that little bit soft on her. But sure what she want with an old mongrel the like of me? In the end, anyway, Redmond, she went off and married a doctor. Lives in England or someplace now, I hear. But a lovely girl she was all the same. Now where in the divil did I put that jug of clear?

It was a masterful performance and there is no doubt about it. He could simply, effortlessly, run rings around me. And I know that, although maybe it's not something to be particularly proud of, there have been many times since that day I called to the house and collected Immy when I would have given anything to have possessed even a *fraction* of Ned Strange's formidable resourcefulness. The tiniest percentage of his linguistic dexterity, the meagrest portion of his adroitly evasive, exculpatory strategies.

Labyrinthine schemes and plans, always presented with a big, open countryman's honest face. They were as natural to the man as eating or breathing. Beside him in these respects I was a pygmy, an ingénu. A minion of no worthwhile consequence. Even just thinking about it humiliated me.

I mean, I could see how efficiently he would have conducted himself on such a day as that appalling one in Deep Pan Pizza. When I'd been stupid enough to stop the car. I could imagine just how effortlessly he would have dealt with such a dauntingly difficult situation – skilfully sidestepping each successive challenge. Encountering Piper Alpha wouldn't have posed a problem in the slightest. Right there on the spot, without even having to think, he'd have concocted some perfectly plausible story, some wryly amusing anecdote which would have validated without question his presence in the restaurant. As opposed to my hapless procession of stuttering maunderings: I'm here to do this, I'm here because of that.

It really is awful to be tongue-tied in that way, and there can be no doubt but that it proved *very, very* much to my advantage indeed that the Scottish oil-rigger happened to be – as he eagerly explained, as though under the impression that we enjoyed some kind of special relationship – leaving for South Africa that same evening.

—Goodbye, Dominic, I heard him calling in the distance.

I thought I'd faint before getting back to the Escort, to the sanctuary of love and my beloved, at last, now slumbering, daughter.

I have never in my life been in need of such resources as I was that day we motored erratically along the highway, my driving at times proving almost as inadequate as my conversational skills. Which, in the end, represented almost a parody of Ned Strange's. To give you an example: instead of remaining calm – twinkly-eyed, even, as he, doubtless, would have done – and launching myself easefully into some devil-may-care narrative, I instead began to relate this detail-heavy version of that day in the park when the two of us had discovered the robin, my hopelessly sentimental disgressions only serving to confuse little Imogen further. It was just so *stupid*, that's the only way I can describe it!

My gestures too – it seems so obvious now – they really were wholly and utterly inappropriate. Much too large and unsettling by far. Operatic, almost, for heaven's sake!

The difference between me and Ned was that it came as second nature to him to act as though he *owned* his audience. Not caring a damn whether you listened to his story or not. Thereby, of course, ensuring that you *did*. That was the paradigm I ought to have emulated.

It was a pitiful performance. I accept that now.

On top of which, I almost crashed the car. Twice. When Imogen's eyes opened I heard her squealing, over the screeching brakes:

—*Daddy!*

Redmond Hatch, the poor man's Ned Strange. All I could say was, if he and I were twins, then I was the weak and ineffectual one. 'Combine with oneself in bold conspiracy'? The idea was laughable. I'd never be Ned Strange.

I simply wasn't up to the task.

Entertain? Why, I couldn't even entertain my own daughter, I remember thinking, burning with shame.

For once upon a time I would have taken her little hand and told her not to be worried in the slightest. About the stupid 'afraid' things or anything else. Would have just squeezed that hand gently, reassuring her after the manner of any ordinary father. Instead of foolishly waving my arms, compressing almost every experience we'd ever had into one single exasperating, quite impenetrable account. Hopelessly over-stimulating the child, who was in a state of extreme anxiety in any case – and, as if that wasn't bad enough, almost killing the pair of us into the bargain. It's pretty obvious now that someone was looking out for us.

—I won't let you down! I could have sworn I heard, at one point.

If only I'd demonstrated some measure of poise. The tiniest approximation of some kind of equanimity. That surely ought not to have been at all difficult, even for someone as ineffectual as Redmond Hatch or Place or Tiernan or Strange or whatever the fuck my name was supposed to be. It really ought not to have been quite so difficult. Even for Redmond the cuckold from the country.

Even for a pathetic mountain mongrel such as me.

2001

Six: Scarlet Ribbons

GEORGE BUSH IS SUPREME in the White House now and the war in the North of Ireland seems definitively concluded. It's hard to believe, I know, but that's what has happened. The world is in a state of flux – constantly changing. That is, and always has been, the essence of being human. *Change*. And life, more than ever now, seems to have altered with a bewildering rapidity – as alien to 'the old mountain-time' as can possibly be imagined. So many transformations since that first journey to winterwood, since that now best forgotten, seriously distressing afternoon.

It all seems so distant at this juncture anyway – once-epochal events possessing no substance, little more now than the dimmest of recollections. Since that time the Rwandan holocaust barely meriting a mention and the slaughtered of Croatia evoking no more than glum shrugs of regret.

As for my life, it too has seen its share of dramatic

transformations – not something you'd expect from drab old 'Redmond Place', the man who can't even translate his own name, it would seem.

But, transformed it has been and – believe you me, having known what it's like to be close to destitute, emotionally and financially – I am very grateful for that indeed.

For a start, I no longer work in the newspaper business, having jumped at the chance when it was offered of a lowly, admittedly, start in the field of television. I really couldn't believe my luck. But the opportunities in Ireland are enormous now, compared to the grim old days of the eighties. And when we had concluded the interview, they told me there and then they were prepared to take me on as a trainee, initially, on a short-term contract. They operated an anti-ageist policy, they told me, and my being in my sixties posed no problem at all. It was changed times in Ireland, I remember reflecting happily. Good fortune has smiled on me practically non-stop since then.

At that time, as I say, my position was modest enough – researching duties, mainly, on the *Primetime* programme – but sufficient to build on, with the result that I now oversee and edit general documentaries and features.

As a matter of fact, I attended the annual television awards only last night in the Burlington Hotel. It was a sumptuously elaborate affair, as has become the norm in affluent Dublin, which misses no opportunity for yet another meretricious fanfare. Casey really enjoyed herself, she told me, and reckoned it was, 'by a whisker', superior to last year's affair.

Casey, by the way, if you've not guessed, happens to be my second wife – and an extremely beautiful lady she is.

Which I'm sure might prove difficult for some people to believe. That someone – someone who's already failed at marriage once, and who isn't in any particular respect striking or remarkable – could ever have succeeded in being so fortunate. Not only to meet but hold on to, I guess, a lady as classy and attractive as the lovely Casey Breslin. To be perfectly honest, there are times when I find it somewhat difficult to credit myself. What's even more exciting is, I have been assured that she loves me. And, even better than that – I believe the woman. Believe her with all my heart.

Even yesterday I could feel it, by the way she held my hand and the look she gave me as we danced. I don't think I've ever been as happy as I am with her. More than with anyone I've ever known before. But then – I've not known all that many women. To be perfectly frank, the only one I really knew, in any depth to speak of, was Catherine Courtney. And Imogen, of course. But you couldn't possibly call her a woman – not at that time, anyway, little kitten. And, in any case, I didn't really know Catherine. I thought I did. But then when she left me for the Maltese, I was compelled to re-evaluate almost everything I'd believed.

—She couldn't have loved you, I'd reproach myself, otherwise she wouldn't have left you for a snake.

Which may or may not have been true – I don't know. All I know is, I'm still fond of her. And always will be. I haven't told Casey that, however. I don't see the point. They are different kinds of loves – with each of them special in their own unique way.

I can't impress upon you how depressing it was, coming upon Catherine's picture so often in the paper. Not to mention the main evening news. And seeing our wedding photo, with my own fuzzy image extrapolated, my eyes already fixed on our blissful future together. That picture of me in that old monkey suit – it looked nothing like me now, of course. Not that it mattered much after the police inquiries had led them to Bournemouth and the anticlimax that was my choreographed 'suicide'. With it soon becoming just another 'tragic case'. Which, in its way, was a very apt description. If not for the reasons which everyone else thought. I had a rather different view of that tragedy.

As far as my apprehension went, I knew being found out was probably highly unlikely. The only one who could possibly have known anything was Piper Alpha. And he had long since departed for South Africa. No one else but him had even been aware of my presence in Ireland. And Dominic Tiernan at sixty years of age, with his grandad shirts and ponytail, didn't look remotely like Redmond Hatch.

In the end everything grew quiet and that suited Imogen and me just fine.

—A beautiful calm on winterwood settled, as the poet might say.

*   *   *

The next time I saw Catherine's photo, in the *Evening Herald*, to say I was shocked would be putting it mildly. But, as it transpired, it had nothing, specifically, to do with Imogen. It was connected to a report of a traffic accident in which her partner Ivan had been critically injured. The headline read: 'Renewed Heartbreak for Mother of Missing Girl'.

I kept a watchful eye on proceedings (it had mentioned in the paper that he'd been taken to St Vincent's Hospital) and, sure enough, Ivan passed away. As soon as I heard the news, I experienced this almost uncontrollable, visceral desire to see her. To the extent that I went back to the pub in Rathfarnham.

It was the saddest of houses now, with people coming and going all day long, paying their respects to her deceased partner, Ivan Lennon. In the little apple orchard the tractor tyre swing just hung there limply, the leaves beneath it crackling and dying.

There was a scarlet wreath on the door and – disrespectful though it might have been – I simply couldn't prevent it from reminding me of winterwood.

Disrespectful, I mean, in the sense that I was indulging in my own pleasure when right there in front of me people were experiencing real heartbreak and trauma. But they had always looked so beautiful, those ribbons – just fluttering away amongst the pines in the dark, where I'd tied them to some branches the first night we'd arrived, and told her how my own mother had used to sing it. 'Scarlet Ribbons', I mean. I just couldn't stop

143

myself dwelling on it. I know what some people might think. That I invented a story to elicit sympathy, even love. Which I needed so badly I would do anything to get it.

But they can think what they like. I don't have to resort to pathetic strategies like that. I know what love is. If I want love it's there in one sentence: the beautiful days we spent in Kilburn.

I washed Immy's bag and brought it out to her. I was shocked when a mini-beast wriggled out of her sleeve but it didn't infuriate me – not the way it might once have done. I just picked it up gently and laid it on the ground. Then the two of us sat there together, and I stroked her fleecy hair in that old warm Queen's Park way. There was a snowfall that night and it seemed so perfect I didn't bother going home at all. The next morning when I got in, I reassured Casey by telling her I'd been working through the night. She said:

—You watch it now, Dominic, or I swear you'll collapse.

—Ha ha, I laughed, and gave my wife a hug.

After Ivan died, Catherine sold the house in Rathfarnham and moved – to where, I didn't know. I went out one day and she was gone. I won't pretend it didn't surprise me. For all my surveillance and clever conspiracies, I hadn't foreseen that eventuality, had I?

I think she must have sold it for a song.

I'd sit in the pub across and think about the days, those long ago days when they'd stand there snipping roses and

Imogen would laugh as Ivan told her some joke. Once or twice after closing time, although I knew it was foolhardy, I climbed in over the garden gate, and sat there in the tyre, thinking – thinking about the Snowman walking in the air, walking in the moonlit sky.

Apart from being with Casey, there was nothing I really liked better than driving out to winterwood. Trying to explain my predicament to Imogen – and somehow justify my embarrassing behaviour that day in the car. One thing's for sure – I'll never shout at her again. I never meant to, anyway. But the Ribena kept spilling all over the seat. I know it's all over now, and it makes no difference, but more than anyone, it's still Piper Alpha I blame. Even now I can remember the awful fright I got, when I looked up and saw him making his way towards the counter. Clapping me on the back and looking at me in that sickly, ingratiating way.

—Hey there, Dominic! Are you on your way back tae the hostel?

—Jesus! I remember crying.

He towered above me, swinging his shoulder bag. You could see he was feeling real pleased with himself. He wasted no time in informing me why.

—Are you going back tae the hostel, Dominic? Well, good luck tae ye! For I'm not. I've got everything packed and I've bought my ticket. You won't be seeing me again in a hurry. I don't know why I ever came to this country. Pissing rain all the time. I'm off to South Africa, mate. Pal o'mine says you can pull in a grand a week down there. A grand, no problem, working in construction. That's where you should go, mate. No point, if you ask me, in hanging around here.

All I could hear was Capetown and Jo 'burg and Jo 'burg and Capetown.

That's right, I remember thinking, there is no point in hanging around here, Piper Alpha. You're correct. Now will you just get out of my fucking way!

Later that night, when Imogen and I were crossing the stream, making our approach to the copse of pine, I remember being almost completely overpowered by the thick sickening smell of spearmint. It's disgraceful the way the water has turned pink – a result of the toxic effluent they allow to be pumped into it – and I can't for the life of me think why the environmentalists haven't come down on Rohan's Confectionery like a ton of bricks.

There wasn't a soul about the place. The squat grey functional building was silent and desolate. All you could hear was the sound of the river flowing. The cloying smell as it wafted on the breeze.

I ran my fingers through Imogen's hair. I had read reports of dead fish in that river – and looking at the thick glutinous texture of the water, it didn't come as any surprise at all. I felt like rasping into Ned Strange's face:

—So this is the something dreadful then, is it? Well somehow, I'm afraid, it doesn't seem quite so bad to me!

As I made my way through the trees, ranged all about me like stern but not unsympathetic guardians, I slowly slid to my knees, the light above me refracting through the

146

branches, as I lifted Immy's soft limp arm, placing it tenderly around my neck, as of old.

I'll often sit in winterwood for hours, eating pizza or Bacon Doubles, or maybe just humming a few bars of 'Scarlet Ribbons', watching all the little ribbons as they flutter in the breeze.

In the timeless beauty of our winterwood home.

2002

Seven: A Blissful Marriage

C ASEY AND I HAVE lived in Sutton on the north side of the city for over six months now. In a fabulous new apartment block, a gated community with twenty-four-hour security, complete with its own terraced garden and mock-marble fountain. You couldn't ask for pleasanter surroundings. And the neighbours are wonderful – they mind their own business and the only time we ever see them is when we have our quarterly meeting about service charges and various other day-to-day management matters. It cost us a packet – over two million euro, in fact – but it's been well worth it. It really has. So I wasn't sorry, leaving my one-room apartment in Ballsbridge. I don't know what I've done to merit such consistent good fortune. I certainly wouldn't have expected this outside a church on Harold's Cross Road one wild and windswept desolate day when all had seemed well and and truly lost. Before, I suppose, you could say I 'yielded'. And brought myself, as a consequence, untold good fortune and constant opportunity. But *love* more than anything. Love with Casey, my darling, loving wife.

I mean, I know I was lucky in the first few years with Catherine – buying Imogen the coat and everything, lifting her up on to the bright, chiming carousel but, despite all that, I never felt loved. Not really – not in the way a man *should*. It's kind of hard for me to admit that now but it's true. I think for a long time I'd been deluding myself. Certainly up until the day when delusions no longer became sustainable. When I found her in bed with her Maltese friend. And was left with no option but to take her aside and say, to enquire of my somewhat flushed and startled wife:

—Well then, Catherine, tell us: *was he any good?*

You shouldn't have to say things like that. Not to your spouse. And wouldn't – certainly not if you thought you were loved. And living with someone who had made it clear on more than one occasion that they didn't, deep down, have faith in you.

All I know is I won't ever be put in that position again. And, believe me, that's a rare and pleasant feeling. Why, sometimes Casey and I – we won't even have sex. We'll just lay there and chat and hold hands like a couple of kids. I've never met anyone who knows me so well. And that, I'm convinced, is the secret of true love. Knowing someone – *especially* knowing and accepting their faults – *that's* the essence of the thing we call love. You don't have to have sex to prove that you're in love. Sometimes I won't feel like it, having worked hard in the office all day. And does Casey say to me:

—Dominic, if you don't mind – I've been seeing someone behind your back. It's this urge, you see, this irresistible attraction I have to *snakes*. I'm sorry, of course, but I'm sure you'll understand.

Nope, that's not what happens. Because Casey Breslin doesn't think like that. Once she loves you she loves you and that's it. That's just the way she happens to be.

—What of it? she'll say instead, we can always make love tomorrow night, Dominic.

Before kissing me on the cheek and turning out the light.

I would use one word to describe our lives together. One single word: *blissful*. That's the word I'd use to describe it.

I never thought it possible for two human beings to arrive at such a level of happiness. One as close to *complete* as any person could dream of.

To give you an example: one night when I happened to be in the throes of expatiating about – I mean, can you believe it? – Ned Strange!

I wouldn't blame you if you thought: Oh, no, not him again!

I'd had more to drink, I suppose, than I ought to and was rambling on at length, I know. But what does Casey do? I couldn't believe it, but there she was, hitting me over the head with a rolled-up magazine. Thumping me repeatedly with a copy of *Hello!*

—Oh, you and those old stories! she complained. Sometimes I think you ought to go back to that old mountain you talk so much about! Get over it, why don't you!

As you can imagine, when I heard her saying that, it

would be something of an understatement to say I was taken aback. But she was right, of course. Ned and the mountain were history and shouldn't have been referred to in any capacity at all. I mean, he hadn't entered my thoughts – why, literally – for years.

Which, of course, tells its own tale.

Once the stress within me had ended – *very mysteriously* – not another word from Ned. Not so much as another single whisper. It was clear to me now I'd imagined the whole episode. And the idea of actually having *seen* him – well, it was worse than embarrassing.

—If I were to wake up and lay eyes on Ned Strange now, I found myself saying, I almost certainly would burst out laughing.

As far as I was concerned, Auld Pappie from the valley didn't matter any more. He'd faded, like his so-called ancient lifestyle, into the receding mists of history. I suppose it had taken Casey to make me see that. By making it plain, once and for all. Saying it straight out in the way that she had.

—He's gone, I laughed, and she swatted me playfully again with the *Hello!*, the old fucker's gone! Good luck, Auld Neddy!

All of which gave me a great kick, I have to say, it being, I suppose, so uncompromisingly decisive and *final*. But Casey really administered the *coup de grâce*. She tossed away the magazine and sighed as she draped herself across the arm of the easy chair: thrusting out her bosom as she fixed me – rather disapprovingly, I have to say – with her gaze.

—I can't for the life of me think why you ever let him

154

prey on your mind in the first place. I never understood why you carried those stupid cuttings in your wallet. Maybe you were guilty about turning your back on your roots, I don't know. But I'll tell you this: you can forget about that sonofabitch. Forget him now, and forget him good. You got that, honeybun?

—I got it, I told her. You won't have to say it again. Message received loud and clear.

—Come here to me, tiger.

I took her in my arms and kissed her right there. I loved her more than ever now, for being so resolute and talking such sense. Of course, it ought not to have come as any surprise. Casey had been born in upstate New York – Albany – and wasn't known for mincing her words.

—No more about that inbred hillbilly, she said and I laughed. I laughed till I was nearly blue in the face.

—Call him that again, I pleaded, say it again, Casey!

I felt so empowered I was almost delirious.

—Hillbilly! Hillbilly! she laughed and so did I.

We were just so stimulated after the wine.

—Fucking inbred! I laughed again, intoxicated by the way she said it, in that strong and confident – but most of all, *urban* – American accent.

We spent that whole night making love. It was fantastic. It really was something. Something else entirely, believe me.

I'm embarrassed to admit it, but before I met her I knew precious little about things like that.

Catherine and I – well, not to put too fine a point on it –

we'd always been somewhat conservative, really. Sexually, I mean.

So that was another remarkable transformation in my life, and it was gratifying. At that stage of my life, to be so *privileged*.

—Aren't you ever going to go to sleep? I remember her saying afterwards.

I laughed when she said it and kissed her neck, pushing up against her buttocks with my 'raging tallywhacker', as we called it when imitating Strange.

Then I laughed heartily as I turned out the light.

It was wonderful, just wonderful, to be living with such a strong woman. If anyone was like two peas in a pod, it was us – me and Casey Breslin, my wife. Because, contrary to what most people might have assumed at the time, when Catherine and I were together, it was old muggins here who had been the dominant partner.

Until things began slowly to unravel. After the incident with the Maltese. After I'd shouted at Imogen over the paints. I had shouted at Catherine too, occasionally, when we'd started having arguments over having another child. I admit that, and deeply regret it. Once even going so far as to say:

—You are treading on very thin ice here, my dear.

Frightening her, I know. I could see it in her eyes. After that, she had always seemed edgy. It must have been the way that I said it or something.

But I was always sure to make up for it in whatever small way I could. The polly pocket I had bought for Immy – she

156

nearly lost her mind when we opened it. It more than compensated for my intemperate outburst. There were lovely little lights and lanterns inside the small plastic open-out toy, all painted up in these adorable pastel colours. And a tiny reindeer the two of us christened Rudolph.

—Look at Rudolph, she said, he thinks he's the boss!

All the other deer were standing around, as Rudolph gazed proudly from his snow-covered outcrop, proudly surveying his almost spectral kingdom, stately and noble in his forest of pine.

Imogen just loved snuggling up to you when a story was over. We made them up as we went along. Winterwood was the most magical place anyone could imagine – a crystal palace carved out of ice, bounded by rows of stiff-standing pines. All streaked with silver and stamped with lovely patterns of frost. It was there the snow babies would make their beds each night, with no one to care for them but each other.

She especially loved the bit about the little robin. The children all pointed at him, crying out as he looked down from his branch.

—Look! Snowboy called, the poor robin is crying!

Her appealing, beautiful little eyes.

—Will we love our robin and keep him safe for ever? she pleaded with me.

—Yes, I reassured her. For ever and ever. Safe for ever in his winterwood home.

—I love it here, she said, with a luxurious little shiver, I love it and want to stay for ever and ever. It's cold but yet it's warm. It's funny, isn't it? I love it, Daddy.

157

I used to love her calling me Daddy. I wish I'd never said anything to Catherine. I wish I'd never mentioned baby Owen. I wish I'd just been happy with what we had. I wish my insecurities hadn't driven her away. I wish I hadn't harped on about baby Owen. I knew it was old-fashioned, being obsessed in that way with the male line. It was like something you'd hear them going on about on the mountain.

If only I hadn't loved her so much or been so suspicious. Maybe if I'd been able to train myself. Then maybe none of those arguments would ever have happened. And our happy little family would still be in Kilburn.

Casey and me, we rarely argued at all, I have to say, and when we did it was generally light-hearted. I couldn't believe my luck when I met her. For a start she was a good two inches taller than me, with her long blonde hair streaming down her shoulders. She was tipped for great things inside RTE. The job she'd set her sights on was overall head of the current affairs department. That was what she wanted and I didn't have any doubt that sooner or later she'd end up getting it.

It came as a surprise to some people that we'd ever got together at all. Not because there was anything particularly wrong with me but because it was well known that for a number of years she'd been conducting an on-off love affair with James Ingram, a foreign-affairs correspondent who was almost legendary in the station. Not least for the reputation he had for seducing women. Maybe that was the reason their relationship in the end had come to nothing. I can't say for sure, though. On the one or two occasions when I had tentatively quizzed her about it, she'd become uncharacteristically irritable and quite snappy.

—Was James Ingram a philanderer? I'd asked her bluntly.

—Oh, what of it! I remember her dismissing it. Some men just can't seem to grow up, that's all!

Whether or not that was supposed to be a compliment indirectly directed at me, I'm afraid that's how I chose to interpret it. It's not every man can boast of a woman as desirable as Casey Breslin selecting them over others. When, in your heart and soul, you know she could have had anybody.

The great thing about love – if it's the genuine article and not some weak imitation – is that every single piece of you is known. You surrender yourself and just hope that you are loved. In the initial stages I'd found it quite difficult, not having been with anyone to speak of – not really, unless you count prostitutes – since Catherine. For a while, in the very early days, I'd been annoying Casey, pestering her with endless questions.

Little niggly things like: 'Really? How much?' And: 'Are you still sure that you will always love me?'

Which really must have been infuriating at times.

But, gradually, over time, I grew into our relationship, privately and somewhat triumphantly, I admit, accepting that she genuinely meant what she had said.

There are some things in a marriage that are best left unsaid. It's hard for me to believe now that I told Casey the truth –

about finding the silver tinfoil in the living room and sensing a definite presence in our bedroom one night. Most of all I find it hard to believe that I told her about the dream, and in such detail. I suppose it was so frightening that I couldn't have prevented myself even if I'd wanted to. It was the most awful dream I think I've ever had. Ned was standing there in that old familar way, but this time he was completely naked. He opened his hand but there was nothing inside. Then he sighed and said softly, almost kindly, in fact:

—The shop had no chocolate, Redmond.

When I looked again he was wearing Immy's bag. It was draped across his shoulder and he was fiddling with it, laughing. He opened it and shook out some ants.

—Naughty! he said, but in Imogen's voice.

I should never have said anything to Casey about it. However, the fact is I did. Because when you're in love with someone that's what you do. Especially when they're so beautiful and intelligent. I had even shown her the photograph – the one I'd snipped from the *Sunday Independent*. The sign ROHAN'S CONFECTIONERY was a little bit blurred but you could see the river curving close by the copse of pine. It was only when I mentioned him whispering 'something dreadful' that her manner began to change quite dramatically. She spun away from me and crumpled up the cutting. She was white.

—People don't come back from the dead, Dominic, she snapped, I mean, for Christ's sake, darling, what on earth are you talking about? I thought that we had cleared this up. I mean, I thought we had been through all this before!

She took a cigarette from her handbag and lit it with trembling fingers. Then she said:

—Look, I don't want to go causing any trouble between us.

I made it clear she didn't have to worry about that. I found myself looking at her and thinking: God, how I love this woman.

—Look, she continued, I don't understand what kind of pressure you were under when you lived in Portobello. What was going on in your Drumcondra days. All I know is – I don't want to hear you ever mentioning it again.

For a minute or two afterwards she remained a little annoyed. But not for very long, I'm glad to be able to say. Then she came and sat in my lap, holding her glass as she looked into my eyes. I stared right back into hers. They were a gorgeous polished hazel. I was putty in her hands.

—You're not offended, she said, with a lovely smile, by my speaking my mind? About you and this – Ned Strange?

—Of course not, I replied, of course I'm not. Who cares about him?

I didn't wait until the next morning. I made up my mind right there and then. And the minute she had gone to bed I gathered up everything pertaining to Ned Strange, every single notebook and tape and paper cutting, then took them out into the garden and burnt them. They included the drafts of my book *In Old God's Time: My Mountain Memories* by Edmund Strange, 1980–82, as related to Redmond Hatch. They were the first to go. The very last image I saw catch fire was one of him appearing, on the day he'd been convicted, outside the Four Courts, shrinking from a

161

baying crowd, with the single word EVIL rubber-stamped across his face.

The sense of relief after destroying the material was enormous. Not since the day of my wedding had I felt so indomitable, so irrepressibly optimistic. It worked wonders for me and Casey too. Things between us had never been so good. She was going from strength to strength now in her career – as indeed, I was myself. The great thing was that we hadn't allowed it to cause difficulties. We'd had the good sense to nip it in the bud. Because what we understood was that love can conquer everything. People can get over anything. She really brought out the best in me, Casey Breslin. She had civilly requested me to do something for her and, as her husband, I had complied. *Fait accompli*, no problem at all. *Au revoir*. So then, Ned, good luck and goodnight. To you and all your partners in hillbilly heaven.

What had happened between me and Casey was a classic example of two people combining their resources, and working together towards an almost perfect end.

Of course, everything wasn't absolutely 100 per cent – it never is between two married people. No, there were the usual predictable arguments, but there are very few people in TV and the world of entertainment generally who don't undergo those from time to time. Especially those with a propensity for high achievement. Which we both possessed, without a doubt, and I, Dominic Tiernan, a once dim bulb, I was learning from Casey every single day.

I used to marvel at the effortless manner in which she

seemed to be able to work a room. They were absolutely mad about the woman in RTE. The irony being that soon after I'd dispensed with all of the folklore rubbish, I was called into the Director General's office and asked if I'd be interested in producing and directing a television documentary, the subject of which was to be – I couldn't believe my ears – the traditions and history of Slievenageeha Mountain!

—Your own home place, I understand, he said.

—Yes, I replied shakily, as the back of my neck began to tingle.

He proposed calling the documentary *These Are My Mountains*, which I told him I considered an excellent title, suggesting we might use Brian Coll on the soundtrack – a singer whom I knew had been a long-standing favourite of Ned's.

—An excellent idea, he said, and gave me a smile, declaring good-humouredly as he rose to his feet that he'd clearly picked the right man.

—For you obviously know your country music!

2006

Eight: May You Never

THESE DAYS I HAVE a tendency to chastise myself for my clumsiness and hopelessly embarrassing lack of tact when announcing my decision to leave RTE. But the truth is that it could hardly have been handled in any other way. I mean, after all, it wasn't Casey who had walked out on *me*. Regardless of what she might have done, irrespective of how despicable her behaviour might have been – and that was pretty despicable, believe you me – it would always be Redmond Hatch who had done the walking out.

Redmond Hatch who, in the February of 2004, had abruptly and dramatically ended the marriage. Or 'flipped', which was how they had taken to describing it in the RTE canteen. I never commented. All I wanted was to get out of the place. Once and for all, just get away. Those were the feelings I had at the time. So there's no point in looking back and trying to rewrite history.

The kind Casey Breslin was, she'd have been able to lie her way out of it anyway, charm judge and jury with that great big disarming Albany smile. There was this way she had of smoothing back her hair. Of lifting up those hazel eyes. You'd pretty much have believed anything Casey wanted you to. A very, very smart lady indeed. All I can say is – she saw *this* fool coming.

I ought to have known the night we were drinking and I asked her to put on the blue dress I'd bought for her in town that day. It really was the most gorgeous dress, and I knew it would look lovely with the matching cornflower-blue hair clasp. But Miss Sophisticate was having none of it.

—I'm not wearing that Pollyanna rag, she snapped – and I had to pretend that the whole thing had been a joke, which of course it hadn't been at all. I'd been thinking of her in it practically all week, after I'd spotted it by chance in the window.

—What's wrong with you? she'd continued, quite unreasonably. It's like something you'd see in the nineteenth century!

She went off to her friend's and didn't phone. And the following day said nothing at all about it. All I kept thinking as I waited for her to phone was: Something dreadful is going to happen.

She came back the following evening, but when I took her in my arms to make love, she moved away and said she was tired.

The only reason I was in a position to leave RTE at all was that around that time the Department of Transport had introduced new legislation with regard to taxi deregulation. Before that, a plate would have cost close on sixty grand, whereas now I was able to get my hands on one for a little under seven. I won't say it saved my life – it's not like I was on the breadline or anything – but it sure as hell made things a damned sight easier.

What I couldn't believe were Casey's sweet smiles when the two of us parted for the very last time. It was as if nothing much had happened at all – apart perhaps from a minor disagreement.

—Bye, darling! she said with a wave, see ya! *Ciao*!

For a while afterwards, I succumbed to bitterness and started drinking far too much. I'd begin in the morning and carry on all day. It would be just like old times, staring out of windows in Temple Bar pubs, surrounded by loud nurses and roistering, invasive students – cowed by the hegemony of hedonism and imperious youth. I was sure I was going to end up in a hostel again, longing to be reunited with Catherine Courtney – the only woman for Redmond Hatch.

Initially, that was a conclusion that had frightened me – I won't deny it. But the more I became acclimatised to it, the more acceptant I became. Knowing that, sooner or later, we would meet again. We were fated to, our two lives fixed on courses which must inevitably intersect. In case I had ever begun to doubt that, one day, quite out of nowhere, Ronan Collins the drivetime deejay introduced a record dedicated to a girl from Cork. Which might have meant nothing, obviously, except for the particular music track which had been chosen. The warmest feeling stole over me then. Obviously Ronan could have played any song. But he hadn't. He had played *that* one. Which I hadn't heard on the radio for years.

Just hearing it changed everything.

Now I was *certain* the two of us were going to meet. And that private inner conviction – well, it just kept me going. Transformed me, in fact, made me more amenable and relaxed in myself.

It was lovely, thinking about Imogen as I cruised along, thinking about Imogen who I'd be seeing later that evening. A stag party reveller in a hat and purple wig gave me a wave from a rickshaw and cheered, before hurtling off into the mass of jostling colour, beaming like a kid as he held on to his hat, as if jaunting through the gates of Eden itself.

It really is great to work in Dublin now. And, operating out of Aungier Cabs in Aungier Street, I have myself an absolute ball. There are eight of us on call here in the control office at any one time – and, generally speaking, we pull together well. I think, in the main, because we're all married men. Occasionally you'll get young whippersnappers, bragging about nightclubs and all the women they've had. But we never take much notice, just laugh it off, like you do if you've any sense. Young blood – it never changes. A few knocks is the thing to shut them up. As we well know. For, all of us taxi men, we've been through the mill. Most of us have been hitched once, if not twice, and are well aware that the only cure is time. And the more time you give it the better for you. I'm only beginning to realise that now. What you've got to do is remain relaxed – try not to be unnecessarily alert or over-anxious. That really is so important. I mean, it's only lately I could accurately describe myself as in any way 'settled' – with regard to my emotional state, I mean. In a way that you could comfortably describe as 'content', or something approaching such a frame of mind. I don't think you really know yourself at all, until you're in your fifties. That's to say: when you've a little experience tucked under your belt. But more to the point, the wherewithal to deal with it. And I think it's only fair to say that, approaching sixty-five years of age, I have that now.

The great thing about cabbing is that, essentially, you're your own boss. I mean, obviously, you're accountable to the office and everything but, by and large, what you do is up to you. You don't want to pick up a fare, well so what. There's no one going to twist your arm.

I woke up one night and there definitely was someone in the room. My heart was beating rapidly and I kept on thinking: He's in here. *Now!*

I knew it was stupid and irrational and all the rest. But still, try as I might, I couldn't shake the conviction off. I could even get the faint smell of damp.

There's something in here! There definitely is – I can feel it! I kept on thinking. But no one came.

And I was fine the next morning.

Nine: Together Again

IT WAS THE 23RD of September 2004, at exactly three
o'clock, when I was coming out of the Royal Dublin Hotel,
having just assisted an elderly American lady with her
luggage, that the most wonderful event, certainly since the
birth of my daughter, took place. In a manner that was
totally unexpected, and yet in a strange way not unexpected at all. Seconds beforehand, I had experienced what I
suppose might be called a presentiment. I mean it was that
real, that *tangible*. I could scarcely breathe, and it was as
though my entire body became covered in scales. Catherine
was standing at the taxi rank across the street, burdened
down with two heavy bags of shopping. She looked so tired,
absolutely drained. The fare I had at the time was an
American lady by the name of Karen Venner and I realise
now she was deeply shocked and taken aback by what she
considered an unwarranted display of unforgivable rude-
ness, which was most likely what imprinted my description
on her memory.

173

—Yes, is all I remember saying, yes, now will you please just pay me the money and go! as I literally flung her bags on the pavement outside the door of the Royal Dublin Hotel.

I couldn't stop shaking and thinking about Catherine, thinking about how she was so *close*, just so *near*.

And, as I'm sure I don't have to tell you, my heart at once went reaching out to her.

I know that some people might say that's a lie, like something you'd expect Ned Strange to come out with. That my heart possessed two unique chambers, and if one of them was warm, then the other most certainly wasn't. But it isn't a lie.

Of course it's not.

—Catherine, I sighed, my darling Catherine.

This is an enchanted day, I kept thinking to myself, these are truly 'the enchanted days', as I turned the car around, away from the startled Karen Venner, and pulled up beside her, tugging my cap well down over my eyes.

Every Christmas it is traditional for the taxi drivers to throw a party for the children of St Jude's Orphanage, the school on the north side for which we often drive. Each one of the cabbies always makes a point of bringing a present, so I went into town to purchase mine. It was a beautiful day, the sort I really love, crisp and clear with everyone in mufflers and coats with furry collars buttoned up to the neck. They seemed pretty certain that it was going to be a white Christmas. At any rate, the major chain stores didn't need any convincing, with Irving Berlin's famous tune piping out of every doorway.

I'll never forget that first Christmas in Soho, not just for the fairy-lit carousel, which, incidentally, had been chiming the tune 'White Christmas' as well, but for the warm and lovely feeling that pervaded Soho itself.

People will tell you the English are remote, but at social gatherings I've often found them anything but – charming in an admittedly diffident fashion, but always more than willing to partake in party games and sing-songs. There appeared to be one in every pub that we passed.

—Everyone's enjoying themselves, aren't they, Daddy? I remember little Imogen saying as she trembled. Trembled with an almost uncontainable delight.

I remember I had arranged to meet Catherine in the French House in Dean Street and when Immy and I arrived, we were delighted to see she was already there. Looking gorgeous in this snow-speckled muffler with a great pile of presents sitting at her feet. As soon as she saw me she strolled across and kissed me. Then, would you believe, who walked in, only a quartet of red-cheeked happy choristers!

That was the first Christmas that meant anything to Imogen. Before that she really didn't have much of a clue. She did now, though. All she could talk about was: 'Christmas, Christmas, Christmas'.

—My friend Emma, she's getting a My Little Pony, she told me, if not once then at least a dozen times.

After that the first chance I got I went straight into Hamleys and purchased one for Santa's sack. Pinkie Pie Pony was all painted up in Day-Glo colours, with a great flowing mane of the glossiest baby pink. She even had these silly coy eyes, with ridiculously long black curly eyelashes. All the kids were going crazy for them then. I hid it safely under the stairs. That night I had the daftest dream: the buoyant theme tune playing as me and Immy rode across the sky, passing the Care Bears as we sailed past the sun.

—Look over there, Pinkie Pie! It's your friends the Care Bears! I heard Immy shouting as she held on for dear life to My Little Pony's streaming mane.

I had been unsure what to buy as my present for the St Jude's Orphanage raffle – so, straight away, the minute that Pinkie Pie came into my mind, I thought to myself: Why not? As a matter of fact, I decided to buy two: one for Immy and one for the raffle.

—So how are we today? the assistant quipped cheerily as she wrapped up the Christmas gifts. Enjoying the festive season, are we?

—We certainly are, I replied with a smile, are you?

—Oh, yes, sir. Yes indeed. They say this Christmas is likely to be white.

—It's looking that way, I said to her, as I lifted my nose and inhaled with delight.

When I was coming out the door, I almost collided with a group of revelling Icelanders, laden down with boxes and parcels. We all apologised at the same time before being swallowed once more by the throng.

And what a glorious throng it was.

*   *   *

Dublin had changed so much, I thought to myself, even since those burgeoning days of the early nineties, when Temple Bar had been little more than a cluster of empty warehouses inhabited by drunken derelicts and wan, impoverished actors. The glistening steel spike that had replaced the long-since demolished pillar of Admiral Nelson seemed to defiantly embody the spirit of the new age – pristine, featureless but full of pioneering and resolute spirit. The forelock-touching days of the lowered eyes and the cardboard suitcase, it seemed now as though they'd never existed at all. Or, if they ever had, it had been in some half-known Eastern European country, whose slope-shouldered immigrants we patronised now. The airport was so crowded that at times it seemed only just capable of functioning. A far cry from the days when Catherine and me took our leave at gate B21, along with a couple of other whey-faced stragglers, every bit as crushed and obsequious as their hangdog, bewildered antecedents. Now all that belonged in the realm of memory – cast disdainfully into history's dustbin.

The sense of triumph in the city was palpable, you could feel it renewing itself for further assaults upon the future. In the capital city in the noughties, especially now that it was Christmas, it really was so good to be alive.

When I got back to the base in Aungier Street, what, to my complete and utter amazement, did I find? One of the drivers, as casual as you like, leafing through the pages of my book *Where the Wild Things Are*, as if he owned the damned thing. That one single incident is sufficient to illustrate just how much things had changed – not with

Dublin but with me, psychologically. Once upon a time it would have been very possible – most probable, in fact – that such a situation could have turned extremely unpleasant.

Not now, though. Especially not at Christmas, for heaven's sake.

It didn't matter at all, I reassured him. I knew there had to be a logical explanation. It transpired that, yes, indeed there was. The poor man was apologetic to the point of embarrassment. Which was just as well, for what had I done? I had gone and stupidly inscribed on the inside front cover. And if that isn't bad enough, had been good enough to write my own name as well.

—Love Daddy XX Redmond

It was a tense moment.

—No harm done, I said, zipping up the holdall.

I became aware he was eyeing me like a hawk.

—There we are! I said gaily, slinging the bag across my shoulder.

—I'm sorry about the misunderstanding, he smiled, I would never knowingly interfere with another man's property.

—Of course you wouldn't! I replied cheerily, aren't we all friends here? Striding out the door, chafing the palm of my hand with my keys.

It was a short journey to St Jude's but I was rigid and preoccupied all the way.

—*Fuck it!* I repeated. How could I have been so stupid?

I persuaded myself, however, that in all likelihood it would come to nothing.

—How many Redmonds must there be in Ireland?

I kept on repeating that. But I still wasn't convinced and I knew that I wasn't.

I wanted to stay until the end of the prize-giving but the little crippled boy was more than I could bear. It was all going fine until they lifted him on to the stage.

—Ah, the little dote, said the woman next to me, as they handed him his present.

It was Pinkie Pie Pony in a transparent box. I stammered an excuse and exited out the back, vomiting in a corner of the wide gravelled yard.

After a double vodka in a bar near the school, I climbed in the car and drove directly out to winterwood. It helped me so much, just sitting there knowing my baby was close by, the tears staining my face as I softly hummed 'Ribbons'.

After that incident in St Jude's, I had a horrible dream. Even now I can't bear to think of it. Catherine is there and she's dressed in this ragged, revealing nightie. She's all painted up in a way you'd never have seen her. All I know is I'm lying underneath her and when she leans in to kiss me, I can feel her hot breath and these strange and distant voices starting to sing in an angelic choir 'May You Never', singing it so hauntingly it's more scary than beautiful and then you see why because when you look again it's not her, it's not Catherine, it's Ned. It isn't Catherine, it's

Ned Strange and he's rocking back and forth. Rocking back and forth as he softly whispers in your ear:

—Just remember, like I said – when it happens, you'll *know*!

For the purposes of my RTE documentary, I had made a number of reconnaissance trips back to the valley, and those earliest departures are amongst my most treasured memories. Casey and I had committed ourselves now to having a child and it was that we looked forward to more than anything.

—What will we call him – if it's a boy? I asked her. She shrugged.

—I don't know, she said, somewhat absently.

—We'll call him Owen! I cried enthusiastically.

—Baby Owen, she smiled, patting her – as yet – flat stomach with reassuring warmth: our one and only baby Owen!

She was so good to me in those days. Like a mother sometimes. Which is ironic, what with her being so beautiful and statuesque and desirable and everything. She'd have my clothes all ready in the mornings, even checking my laptop bag for me, knowing if left to myself I'd be sure to omit something. We'd be like a pair of teenagers when she dropped me off at Heuston Station, insisting on accompanying me as far as the train, remaining there right until the departure whistle sounded.

In retrospect, I suppose, I ought to have been a little more perceptive. I should have realised she was trying too hard. But I suppose if you had suggested such a thing at the time, in all likelihood, I'd have stubbornly refused to believe a word.

When Catherine cried out in the back seat that day, just as I turned into Parnell Square, I got such a jolt that it rendered me speechless. For over ten minutes at least, I would say. It was only that I hadn't expected her to recognise me. Certainly not so quickly. Not with the beard and the baseball cap and everything. And it threw me completely, it really and truly did. No one likes lifting their hand to their wife, regardless of whether they're separated or not. The woman you love, the mother of your child. It doesn't matter how many misunderstandings there were.

—Oh, Jesus, Catherine, I really am so sorry, I said.

But her peals of panic turned everything upside down. Why had I done it? I asked myself. You have no idea how rotten it made me feel. She fell across the groceries and slumped across the seat.

—It's going to be OK, darling, I said. You and me and baby Owen and Immy. After this all our problems are over.

Listening to her heavy breathing, somewhat erratic at first but gradually becoming steadier, I started to chat to her and, slowly but surely, it made me feel good. Gradually, in time, coming back to my senses, instructing myself to relax and not to go making the same mistake again. The one I'd made with Imogen, I mean.

So I kept on talking, maintained a constant dialogue, one that was nice and fluid and easeful: I wanted to put Catherine's mind at rest. In the middle of the story I caught a fleeting glimpse of myself in the rear-view mirror and for the first time it dawned on me just how easily, how ridiculously easily, in the baseball cap, I could have passed for Ned Strange. You could see the copper-red curls showing from underneath the baseball cap. Why, I literally could have been the man's twin! I thought.

Which alarmed me momentarily, I have to say, when I considered the prospective effect on passengers. But I was pretty sure, on reflection, that most people by now had forgotten the old idiot. Perverts like him were in the news every day. Ned Strange was just another old relic, a forgotten memory from a country that had more or less vanished, now that the modern world at long last had arrived. There was nothing in the slightest to worry about.

Ten: The Story of Little Red

WHENEVER CASEY WAS AWAY, I'd buy myself a bottle of wine and sit in the conservatory thinking about things. About how far we'd come and how somehow I'd triumphed against all the odds. Which were always going to be stacked against you if you happened to be born in a place like Slievenageeha.

—Home of the inbreds, I laughed as I drank, hillbilly valley!

Reminding myself to say it to Casey as soon as she got home.

—Hillbilly valley! I could hear her laughing as we shared a glass, you sure did well to get outta that place. You did well to abandon them and all their malice, the ludicrous suspicions and hostility towards that great big world beyond their mountain – the civilised world, in other words, my darling. Where fathers and brothers don't fuck their sisters and mothers don't die of brain haemorrhages after being beaten by brutes to within an inch of their poor wretched lives!

*   *   *

—Hillbilly Valley! I'd chuckle when she said it. Even if, somewhere, deep down, it hurt me a little. Because, after all, it was my home. And, whether I liked it or not, I had grown up there. Once upon a time I had been a little boy, had I not, who hadn't had any choice in deciding where he was born. Yes I had – had been a little boy with my own father and my own mother, even if I hadn't lived with them for all that long. The more I thought about it the sadder it began to seem. It was like a sad story that made you want to weep and bawl.

I was glad that Casey wasn't there to see me, as I worked my way through three bottles of wine and, believe it or not, an entire box of Kleenex – which is not something, I'm sure, my wife would have been all that keen to see me doing.

But I was fine by the time she got home. I had managed to get it all out of my system. You'd never guess I'd been thinking long and hard about the story of 'Little Red', a sad weepy tale from a forgotten mountain valley.

This is the story. Little Red lived in the mountain valley. He lived in the valley with his dad and his mam. But then one day it was decided that he wasn't to live with them any more. He was sitting by the fire warming his hands in their cabin when all of a sudden a large shadow appeared and fell across the floor. The little boy was surprised because he hadn't been quite expecting that. The shadow turned out to be that of a priest. In those far-off days it was the custom of clergymen to wear a hat. A great big broad-brimmed special priest's hat. This clergyman was wearing one and carrying a great big leather missal. Its zip was golden. He paused for a second before saying:

—Little Red.

Everyone called the boy that. Although he was sitting by the fire where it was warm he was still wearing his new overcoat. The one with the big buttons and the brown velvet collar. The one which his mother had bought him in Burton's of the city. The priest felt the collar and enquired of him softly:

—Did your mother buy it for you, in Burton's of the city?

Little Red confirmed that yes, indeed she did. She had done that. The priest looked away for a moment and then said:

—Ah.

Before pushing back his big priest's hat. Little Red formed the impression that the clergyman was very tired. He watched him rubbing his face with his soft, unweathered hands. Probably very tired, regularly delivering news of the sort he was about to hear. To the effect that the boy's mother Mrs Hatch wouldn't be dealing with Burton's of the city any longer or Burton's of anywhere for she had just been found dead whilst praying in the chapel.

—Praying at the altar rails, he sobbed, we found her prostrate at the feet of Jesus. She's happy where she is now, my son.

That was the story of Mam Hatch's death. Or as Ned used to say:

—Your version of it, Redmond.

*   *   *

185

It was still on my mind when we set off for the valley the following day to start filming. We arrived at the Slievenageeha Hotel round about six and and I'd gone to bed early, for it had been a long drive and I had to rise at six. The first thing I noticed when I awoke around one was the wide-open window. Which I was absolutely certain I'd closed before retiring. I couldn't for the life of me figure out how that had happened. I went to get a drink but the taps were bone dry. I resolved to mention it to the manager in the morning.

The following night wasn't any better. I woke at three, ice cold and shaking all over. But at least this time there was water in the taps. I had made it my business to make sure of that.

—What in the hell sort of a hotel do you call this? I'd snapped at the manager.

There was a force-ten gale blowing outside. You could see the mountains: rearing like horses before the face of the moon. Flashing their incisors and tossing back their fierce proud heads, ropes of saliva hanging from their pink lips. I did my best to keep my imagination in check. That was a problem I'd had as a boy. I sat on the edge of the bed, steadying the trembling glass in my hand, trying hard not to think about Florian. Being back in the valley had started it all again. I jerked when I thought I had heard his voice. Then I saw his face in the window: winking at me, in that awful way he did, raking his fingers through his mass of red hair. When I looked again, the face was gone.

*   *   *

Everyone loved him, Uncle Florian. There wasn't a tune he couldn't play. Slip-jigs and hornpipes and high reels and polkas. You name it, Florian could play it. He had played at hundreds of ceilidhs. Not just in Ireland but all over the world – in Newfoundland, Cape Breton and Argentina too. There was nowhere him and his fiddle hadn't been. There was also talk of him having lived in America. But that couldn't be confirmed. And Florian wouldn't help. He'd just sit there grinning as he bared his teeth. Bared his teeth and tapped his foot.

There were some people in the valley who couldn't abide him, however. Who judiciously went out of their way to avoid him.

—Malice, you'd hear them whispering in the pub, there's a very bad drop in that wicked bastard. I'd just be afraid it'd travel down the line. That's all I'd be afraid of. Especially now the mother is gone.

Which it most certainly would – if Uncle Florian had anything to do with it.

Well anyhow, the day finally came when the car arrived to take away Little Red, driving him off to the home of Holy Jesus. The home was run by the Nazareth nuns.

—There's damn all option open to me now, now that herself has been taken up to heaven, but to send the little fellow to the nuns in the orphanage, his father offered by way of explanation. For me and Florian, sure we don't understand things the way women does. We're just not fit to look after him any more. Isn't that the truth?

His brother Florian nodded gravely.

—As long as we make sure to visit him regular, he said, then dammit to hell, it mightn't turn out so bad. I'll see that it won't, for I'm the boy that won't forget that little feller. He's a topper, that's what he is. Why, I'll bring him chocolate every week. I'll bring him a dang-sweet bar of chocolate!

—You're a good one, the boy's father replied, and produced the clear to reward his brother.

—We all stick together here on the mountain, he said, and we won't let him down, that young feller of mine.

—Now you're talking! Florian cried. We'll go down to that orphanage every week. And, maybe when things has kind of improved, he'll be fit to come home and live here for ever.

—Back home to the mountain when things has settled!

—Good health! cried Florian, emptying his mug. As a matter of fact I'll visit the boy this very coming Sunday!

So the following Sunday what did the occupants of a certain grey, utilitarian building hear disturbing its tranquillity? What sound came creeping to the good sisters' ears?

Why, the unmistakable screech of Florian's fiddle, as it mimicked the wind with its deep rushing sound.

Florian's oft-stated preferred dance of choice was the hornpipe. He liked jigs and reels – but by and large always plumped for the hornpipe.

—Get up out of that, he'd say with a flourish of his bow, and show your uncle the cut of your heels!

As he sawed out the melody in four-four time. Shoving down copious swallows of the clear.

Throughout the dance, you would notice his eyes, especially when approaching the close of the tune.

—I'm The Twinkletoe Kid! they seemed to say. And you'll dance it, damn you. You'll dance that hornpipe till your fucking heels bleed!

The sisters loved to see him coming. They asked him to play 'The Last Rose of Summer', the Thomas Moore song. And it must be admitted that he played it quite magnificently. It wasn't like the other tunes. It was softer, more lyrical and gentle and mellow. With the notes like drops of water falling slowly in the stillness. Which was why they liked it so much. And why they probably thought that Florian's soul was something similar in texture to its sad drifting heart. They said he was the nicest man who'd ever visited the orphanage. They knew about the rumours but they didn't believe a word. They loved his chat. He told them yarns about places he'd been. They lapped them up. Stories about Cape Breton and America and Argentina. Places they had never been to before in their lives – how would they? They were only ordinary old country girls. Ordinary old country girls who had never left the slopes of Slievenageeha. Never once in their quiet, exemplary lives. Uncle Florian was like something from their dreams. Secret dreams about which they never dared to tell anyone. Never a word about the night-time visitors who would slip from the shadows with dark eyebrows and teeth and something they had which pleasured you – and of which most emphatically you could never speak. That's what they thought when Florian arrived, lifting up his bow to play the 'bowld' Tom Moore. That's what they were thinking of when he'd stroke his chin, stroke his chin and give them a wink. Saying he liked hornpipes – especially with Little Red. They were afraid if they listened to Little Red's stories, especially the ones about being 'scared of the hornpipe', that Florian would disappear and never come back for as long as they lived. So they said to Little Red:

—Button your lip, you moaning little minnie!

And demanded that in future he look forward to Florian's visits. Those Sundays when Florian would say:

—Right, sisters. Me and me nephew is going off for a ramble. I have a few things to tell him about the goings-on at home. A few little bits of private business, you understand.

—Very good then, Florian, the good sisters would say, but make sure to come back to say goodbye before you go.

—I will indeed, sisters, have no fear of that, my dears.

Throwing his arm around Little Red's shoulders as off they went down the slopes into the meadow. Where Florian stamped out his stogie and grimaced. Before grabbing a hold of him and muttering with a grunt:

—Right so, Redmond. In here with us now behind the big tree. This is a good place as any, for you and me to dance our hornpipes. We can dance in here till our fucking heart's content! Get over there now till I get out my fiddle! Till I get out my fiddle, well boys – ah – dear, ha ha!

*   *   *

And such sawing and scraping as would fill the woods then, as the leaping music screeched above the tops of the tall pine trees.

Little Red often thought of 'spilling the beans'. Of telling the nuns the actual truth about Florian's visits. Of informing them just exactly what kind of 'hornpipes' were 'going on' behind that tall tree in the meadow. Hornpipes which included snapping 'likenesses' with his camera.

—I like to snap likenesses with me auld box brownie. The auld box brownie that I bought in America. Lift up your head now and say cheese for Uncle Flossie. Stick your lips out like you're giving mammy a 'birdy'!

Little Red had one of those photos. He'd kept one all his life. The only one which hadn't been vile. But he'd destroyed it in the end, torn it in pieces, one night he'd got drunk.

Little Red knew what the nuns would say. If he decided to 'spill the beans'.

—It's all lies and slander! Why we'll beat you to within an inch of your vicious lying life!

And so he said nothing. Being condemned as a result to dance his hornpipes over and over.

With warm sticky chocolate plastered over his face.

Eleven: It Isn't Hard to Know a Snake

CATHERINE AND ME HAD just left Blanchardstown behind when a shrill, twofold note came floating so airily out of her throat, for all the world like the most timid little bird.

—Like a sweet lonely robin, I remember thinking, the speedometer fixed now at a steady fifty-five. Nothing too dramatic or over-exciting this time.

A little robin so unnecessarily afraid, I thought to myself, so unnecessary, so *redundant*. There were no more 'afraid things' now, I assured her. We're simply going home, I said.

—Did you ever see a robin cry? I asked her, leaning back as I did so, smiling: Did you, Catherine?

I tugged my cap well down when I said it – quite pointlessly, really, for what possible difference could it make now?

Nonetheless it had really thrown me, her alertness, I mean, in recognising me.

—It isn't hard to know a snake, she had said with a

depressing vindictiveness, a vindictiveness which surprised and deeply hurt me.

There are some things which you're better off not hearing, even if people feel them about you.

—Why did you have to say that, Catherine? I asked her. Why? I hope you're not going to spoil things again.

My entire life, my very *soul* depended on our happiness in winterwood now. That was why I had bartered for it. And why I didn't want *anything* to remind us of the bad times we'd had together. But in another way she was right and I knew that. For when you live with someone, you will always get to know so many things about them. I mean, look at all the things I knew about Catherine, the Knickerbocker Glories she liked in the Sunset Grill, the way she hummed John Martyn songs. The only difference being that I *loved* those things and with Catherine that simply wasn't the case. I suppose a part of me still didn't accept it, and that was the reason I kept insisting that I'd changed, trying to collect my thoughts as I drove.

—You'll see, Catherine, the more you get to know me, I said, that it's different now.

And it was true. I was far more chatty and outgoing for a start. But still aware enough not to make the same mistake I'd made with Immy. No unnecessary displays of emotion, I told myself. Take it nice and easy and relaxed. 'Flowing' and 'light-hearted' – those were the words which remained foremost in mind. Casual and relaxed but, more than anything, 'entertaining'. I related a few stories about London after she'd departed, about the early days in the dark Drumcondra hostel. I had learnt so much

– in particular, not to burden a story with detail unnecessarily.

Taking your time in that old Slievenageeha way.

I decided it was better to be frank with Catherine, to be
straight and direct. I asked her straight out what she
thought of my new image. I stroked my curly beard and
grinned at her in the mirror. I swear I was the image of
Uncle Florian and Ned. And, of course, of my own deceased
father. You wouldn't have been able to tell us apart.

—The men of the mountain! I said, just for the laugh.

She didn't answer. She was quiet now, and hostile, like in
those Kilburn days I remembered so well.

She was under no obligation to answer me. Of course she
wasn't. The two of us were adults. It didn't matter anyway.
Kilburn now belonged to the past. There was only one place
that mattered now. Because it's been ordained, I said, two
paths intersecting which should never in the first place have
diverged.

As we approached the factory, I became overwhelmed by
these absolutely fabulous thoughts of 'home' and 'hearth' –
with this one single word appearing in my mind and
obstinately refusing to go away: Pappie.

Auld Pappie.

—Pappie, I kept repeating, adjusting the mirror as I
scrunched up my face, pushing back my copper locks.

I wanted to be the best father. I wanted to be the most
adored father in the world.

Which is funny, of course, because that is exactly what

Ned Strange had always wanted. Deep down now I could see that. And began to feel a renewed compassion for the man. Because it was obvious to me now that much of what had happened, it, plain and simple, hadn't been his fault. A lot of it had been simply bad luck. It could have happened to anyone really. Especially anyone who'd had a difficult upbringing. As many of us on the mountain – regrettably – had.

What they'd done to him in prison had been despicable. They'd urinated in his food, sprayed 'nonce' on the door of his cell. He'd attempted suicide, I'd read, three times. Before, of course, eventually succeeding in the solitary cold of a prison shower cubicle.

Which explained, the more I thought about it, why he'd shown such *concern* for me at times. As though he didn't want me, being a fellow mountain man, ending up being humiliated like that, or made unhappy by women who didn't love me.

We were now approaching winterwood and I was explaining to Catherine how things had changed. How she had nothing to worry about now.

—I've learnt, I told her. I've grown up, you see. Why, I daresay if you were to ask any of my workmates who of us all is the most devoted father, I guarantee you this, they would seriously consider me.

I lit a cigarette and turned the dial to find some music on the radio. I was half-expecting to hear John Martyn. It didn't happen, which I have to say surprised me.

—To give you an example, Catherine, I continued, only last week during the Christmas festivities, the girls from the brothel next door to the office arrived laden down with bottles of champagne. Well, did that cause a stir or what! Larry Kennedy's eyes were out on sticks!

I shook with laughter as I slid into the middle lane.

—Hmm, you look nice, says this hooker to me, and you know I'm not crude but before I know it she's down on her knees and – Catherine, I'm not kidding you! – doing her level best to get me, you know, aroused, quite frankly!

I had to chuckle when I thought of it.

—But there was no way I was going to permit that to happen. Get up – do you hear me? I was on the verge of saying, Catherine. Get up, I told you! What are you – a fucking whore? It was on the tip of my tongue, Catherine! Because, I mean, she was really taking liberties. It was just so unnecessary, and so fucking coarse – you know? An uncomfortable situation, certainly, and one which, at the time, could really have gone either way. Which is where Pappie came in, reliable Auld Pappie. As the whore knelt beneath me, I smiled to myself and thought of good Auld Pappie with his great big twinkly open-hearted smile. Ah, Pappie, I thought, the man with the greater life experience. The man who possesses that little bit of extra wisdom. That little bit that makes all the difference. I touched her gently on the shoulder and laughed as I said:

—Get up out of that now – there's a good girl.

Which in the end saw that no one was offended. Absolutely no one. Even the prostitute was good-humoured about it all, swinging her bag as she flounced off.

—Sorry, big fella. Didn't realise you were such a loyal husband! Ha ha!

It had worked perfectly. If only I'd been privy to such knowledge and self-possession before, I remember thinking, as I heard my name called out, and I strode out the door to collect my fare.

But then, who ever succeeds, in early life, in grasping the fundamentals of such wisdom? What do you know when you're first starting out? You know nothing. You think you're going to get married and that's the way it's going to remain for ever. You believe it when they tell you that such a thing exists as marital bliss. You're overjoyed when you hear that what's facing you is a lifetime of sensation and discovery and loving enchantment of the heart.

—You never pause to think that it might be all lies, I murmured aloud, half to Catherine and half to myself, as I slowed the car and turned in off the road, to where the tall stately pines stretched majestically into the sky.

Twelve: A Bar of Chocolate

So it's AULD PAPPIE Tiernan they call me now, and the name fits me like a glove – I really have grown into it.

—There he is, Auld Pappie! you'll hear them calling, and look, he's in early again! Putting everyone to shame, Auld Pappie, so you are!

I'm always showing them photographs of my kids.

—Every cent goes on his youngsters, they say, dotes on them, he really does.

Although 'likenesses', as Florian used to call his photographs, might be a more appropriate term, since for obvious reasons I can't publicise my actual family.

—This is Cara, she's my eldest daughter, I tell them.

These indeed are the blissful days. Each day when I'm driving through the city I never fail to remind myself just how lucky I've been. How utterly fortunate: unlike poor Ned Strange, whose last days on earth were truly appalling. For how else could you describe the poor man sitting there, minding his own business in the prison yard, reading his westerns and harming no one at all. When, out of nowhere, he looks up and sees this little lean-faced inmate, clearly intent on causing trouble. Staring down menacingly, kicking the book out of Ned's hand.

—It's a good thing to be a nonce, he says, that's a good thing to be, isn't it? It's a good thing to abuse a child. Take away his innocence and then go around acting like you're some harmless old man. We know what you're at, cunt. Using your stories to get them to like you. Conning them up to the two bloody eyes. Sharing your tobacco and playing your poxy fiddle. You're going to get it now, you fucking nonce! You won't walk out of here alive!

It turned out that the little bastard had a spanner underneath his coat. Laying into Ned, with the guards just standing there as if nothing was happening.

I'd read all that in the magazine *Irish Crime*. To be fair, it was quite a reasonable and balanced report. Unlike the tabloids who'd sensationalised everything. Making a skit of how Ned had tried to get the prisoners on his side, convincing them that he'd actually *adored* Michael Gallagher. And hadn't intended any harm to come to him at all.

How could he possibly ever have been attracted to him sexually? he'd repeated constantly, with tears of heart-break flowing down his cheeks. He was just an old man, for heaven's sake, he kept insisting. All he'd ever wanted was a wife and a little child. He would never – *never!* – have harmed little Michael.

—I loved him, don't you understand? he told them. Why can't you understand? He was the star of my ceilidh.

He fed my chickens! I adored Michael Gallagher! I would never have harmed a hair on his little head!

They didn't believe him, however. They told him he was a liar. Went further and insisted that he was lying through his teeth. Then the rumour started about him actually losing his mind. That was what was happening now, it was said. Sitting in the corner muttering to himself, eating bits of paper and trembling. But then it transpired that this too was an act. That all he was doing was laughing at them. That he didn't give a damn about anything they did or said. That he wasn't even afraid of them. That he'd been making fools of them all, all along.

—He used to laugh into my face, one of the warders was quoted in the magazine as saying, he'd stand there grinning and offering you chocolate. 'Michael used to love it, officer, you know,' he'd say. Make you shiver so it would, the way the dirty, creepy bastard stared.

It was a pity the warder had had to see it like that, I thought. I could understand it, though, for I'd once myself thought in the very same way. Would indeed have insisted, without question, that Ned's intentions all along had been to murder Michael Gallagher, with no particular motive at all.

The fact is that to someone like Ned Strange such thinking would have been inherently abhorrent. Certainly without doubt he'd been longing for many years for a family of his own – in particular, as he'd told me on many occasions, a little boy. But he wouldn't have kidnapped a child solely for that reason, to experience what family life might be like, even for a ludicrously short time.

No, that wasn't it at all. Ned Strange had sexually abused Michael Gallagher all right – just as he'd done to another person in a room in Portobello, one night long ago now best forgotten.

—Poor Little Michael, I remembered him saying, as my skin crawled, imagine trusting the likes of me. I suppose it's the chocolate, Redmond, ha ha. They just can't say no to the chocolate, can they, the little bestest friends of Ned?

Thirteen: These Are My Mountains

I WAS VERY MUCH at ease now with the world and with myself. Which is why, when one of the cabbies in the office happened to say to me one day:

—We were wondering, Pappie, if you weren't too busy, might you come along to one of our prayer meetings?

I had no problem at all accepting the invitation.

And why, for months afterwards, I made it my business to attend with regularity, adding my voice to their thriving little congregation. They all kept telling me how delighted they were to have me. I assured them humbly that the pleasure was all mine and that perhaps one day I might bring along my family. Cara, of course, and Owen, my little son.

I told them I was looking forward to the day of Cara's first Holy Communion.

—She'll be seven next birthday, I said.

They agreed it would be a very special day.

Every Sunday after our prayers, we had tea in a little hall. We sat and talked about the state of the world in general.

—Perdition seems to me just around the corner, a sad-eyed old man remarked, nipping a biscuit as he added: I've lived through two world wars and I never thought I'd see things like this. Men of God in this once-innocent little isle. To think of the things they've been accused of doing.

Those lusty old priests and their rampant tallywhackers, I thought to myself.

—It's dreadful, I agreed with him, absolutely dreadful.

—It is, Pappie, he agreed. It's worse than that, I'm telling you. Far worse.

I nodded and laughed ruefully, in that convincing and practised Auld Pappie way.

I always made sure to kneel up at the front, where everyone had a good view of me, thrusting out my chest as I chanted 'Let Me Lie in the Arms of Jesus'. A photograph was mounted of me devoutly praising Our Saviour. Why, I seemed the loveliest old-timer you ever laid eyes on. With nothing but goodness and decency in my heart, undiluted love for the world and its neighbour.

I was standing in the office one day, leafing through a copy of *Homer Simpson's Scrapbook* – I had repeatedly searched the shops and hadn't been able to find anything about *Sweet Valley High* – which I'd just

bought for Imogen, when I overheard one of the
drivers saying:

—It's hard to even get him to come out for a pint.

I received that as a compliment. But didn't acknowledge it. Just smiled warmly, from ear to ear. But then I
heard:

—I wouldn't be so sure about him. I wouldn't be so sure
about that fellow at all.

I immediately froze, but I didn't have to look. I knew
straight away who the commentator was – the driver I'd
caught interfering with my property. It was hard not to
react, I won't pretend it wasn't.

But I was a different man now. Auld Pappie didn't react
in impulsive, foolhardy ways.

—*Ha ha*, I laughed.

And just went off about my business.

The more time passed, though, the more I found myself
brooding over the incident. I became jittery and on edge,
and it grew more difficult to keep up the Auld Pappiness, as
it were. Like the smart-ass cur I had in the car the other
night. Mouthing out of him to impress his intoxicated
girlfriend, so hopelessly drunk she hardly even knew her
own name. I was playing some music and the next thing
you know, what do I hear him saying?

—What's that on the tape, grandpa? What kinda shit's
that you got playing on there?

The girlfriend started laughing. I flipped the cassette
out, and found something modern to keep the morons
happy. But, as I say, it wasn't easy either. I mean, I could

205

just as easily have stuck the car to the road and told the little bastards to get out of the cab.

—Get out of the car this minute, scum!

I could have said that. Or something along those lines. But I didn't. Like I say, I quietly and simply ejected the tape.

—We like Britney Spears, they slobbered.

—So you don't like the country and western music at all! I laughed. You leave the like of that to old-timers such as me!

They didn't reply. Too busy skitting semen on to the back seat.

The song I'd been playing was 'Nobody's Child'. It meant a lot to me, for reasons which I presume are obvious. I often sang it in the cab to myself. It's a lot of old nonsense, they'll tell you about that song – a load of embarrassing sentimental twaddle. It's like 'Snakes Crawl at Night', they'll say. You couldn't possibly go around taking songs like that seriously. I mean, ordinary wives just don't do things like that – simply go off and make love to snakes. Someone like Catherine Courtney might. But not Casey Breslin.

Most certainly not Casey Breslin, sophisticated lady-about-town. But I have to say, the second year we had spent living together, Casey and I – it was amongst the most rewarding of my life.

Once again I was deliriously happy. I just couldn't believe it. Life being so good that anyone observing me that morning on the train to Slievenageeha would have been prompted to remark:

—There are few times in your life when you are lucky enough to witness such a calm and peaceful expression on a man's face. He must be in love. That's all you can conclude.

And it was true – I was in love. Very much so. As was Casey. Blowing kisses after the train, to the husband she so loved and respected and adored.

The theme of the documentary *These Are My Mountains*, which I was off to start shooting, was the rapidly changing face of modern Ireland, how an old, almost ancient, way of life was vanishing in front of our very eyes. The completed film juxtaposed images of the vibrant new valley – in the foreground the Gold Club, a vast glass-fronted nightclub on five floors, bathed in blue light at the foot of the hills, set in the midst of a plethora of business parks and apartment complexes, hi-tech plants and German hypermarkets, the entire place buzzing twenty-four hours a day – against old grainy monochrome footage orchestrated by nostalgic strings. The closing image, in time-lapse sepia, depicting the rugged, magisterial mountain peaks slowly fading into the mist, as though returning to some lush and blistered paradise, an evanescent, primordial Eden, along with them a tumble-down stone cottage, where Florian had gambled far into the night, smiling lasciviously at his nephew as he reached for his fiddle, sawing out wild solos that leapt untamed like screeching gales.

*   *   *

Neither of us expected the extraordinary success which was to come the way of that little documentary, already having moved on to other things. In a way I had seen it as drawing a line underneath the past.

—Slievenageeha, I'd said to myself, sweet and peaceful mountain: *au revoir* for ever.

Even when early indications had seemed favourable – its first outing had been unanimously praised in the papers – I had not attached all that much importance to it. Then one day while working at home I'd received an unexpected phone call from Casey. She excitedly informed me that *These Are My Mountains* had been shortlisted for the Irish Film and Television Awards, and was being tipped in Montrose as very likely to win.

Which was exactly, in fact, what came to pass.

The reception was held in the Westbury Hotel. I could barely stand up when I heard my name called out.

—And the winner is . . . Dominic Tiernan for *These Are My Mountains*, in the documentary and features section.

When I looked up, I could see her clapping through the haze, in a long lamé gown with her blonde hair tied back.

—Dominic! I heard her cry.

Then she was standing beside me, taking my arm and kissing my cheek.

—I'm so *proud*! she told me.

I put my arm around her waist: all of my colleagues were sharing in the moment. The noise of the applause was a triumphant, invigorating storm. It was wonderful.

So much so that it took me a minute or two to focus on
James Ingram. James was tall. About six foot four.
Originally from London. He informed us – with no need
of prompting – that of late he had cut down on a lot of his
foreign travel.

—I'm seriously considering moving out of foreign cor-
respondence altogether, he said, adding: I'm getting too
old, I'm afraid – and that's all there is to it.

Then he laughed and congratulated me again.

—I'm so pleased for you, Dominic! he said, I really and
truly am delighted!

He had a great dignity about him, James Ingram: the
neatly combed silver hair, the cut-glass accent – and those
unflinching, steadfast eyes, reflecting that unmistakable
Saxon sense of self-worth.

—Oh, darling! cried Casey, I'm so over the moon about
all this. I'm like a teenager, I swear. I don't know what to
say!

I smiled and swept a glass of champagne from a passing
tray. If anyone has ever been given a second chance, I
thought, it's me – Dominic Tiernan.

I sipped my sparkling champagne and smiled.

And, best of all, no one ever found out about winterwood, I thought to myself. Our happy home, it remains
unspoiled.

Permitting myself a little private moment of self-con-
gratulation as I thought of that empty Bournemouth
beach, and my clothes so poignantly folded on the sand.
The exhaustive searches of the police having come to
nothing.

To my amazement, however, despite those comforting and reassuring thoughts, the champagne glass began quivering in my hand. A hand that, I successfully persuaded myself, could only be doing that for one possible reason. Not because, for one split second, I had thought I had heard:

—Daddy, I'm cold. Daddy, please, I don't like it up here. Please, Daddy, can I go home now?

But because I was happy I thought of Catherine. I thought of the award. I thought of Imogen, my precious little girl sound asleep, with a scarlet ribbon fluttering softly above her head.

For a second or two Casey appeared uneasy. She pushed back her hair and stared at me intently.

—Dominic? she said.

—Yes, dear? I replied.

—Are you OK?

—I'm absolutely fine, I assured her.

—Are you sure?

—I said I'm fine! Tell me Casey, are you deaf or something?

It wasn't the reply I ought to have given. I knew that. If only Catherine had believed in me, I kept thinking.

But did not dwell on it. For those days were gone. That was the past. It was onwards and upwards now, no place for self-indulgence. There were just too many new heights to be scaled, thanks to this magnificent, truly blessed second chance.

—Casey, I said, as I took my wife's hand.

—Yes, my love?

—I want to thank you for being my wife. I want to thank you for everything you've done.

—My Dominic Tiernan. I love you so much.

Casey was a picture. A lovely living walking dream.

Fourteen: Heaven's Golden Halls

I HAD LAST THURSDAY off so I decided to go drinking. I ended up in a lap dancing club, not far from the Temple Bar area where I spent the whole day quaffing wine, near the restaurant where Rudyard's used to be.

The lap dancing club was lit in dim aquamarine, with ultraviolet strip lighting and swirling staircases panelled in chrome. I was sitting in a corner banquette nursing a whiskey when a blonde in a tasselled bikini arrived over, wiggling her ass. She looked grotesque, with a swipe of lipstick put on with a trowel. The display of 'erotica' continued for a few minutes. Then she leant over and kissed me full on the lips, lifting her breasts and juggling them like fruit. She gave her genitalia a stroke or two before asking me for money. Wondering might I be interested in the privilege of an even more exciting, more intimate dance? I was on the verge of asking might she be interested in the privilege of getting herself hurt and perhaps hurt very badly, when, out of nowhere, I heard this voice which I recognised at once as Larry Kennedy from the base.

His arrival was fortuitous for I was in no mood for talking to strippers, especially not anaemic-looking wretches from Eastern Europe or anywhere else. He signalled that he and his friends wanted to join me. I beckoned them over and ordered a drink right away. His companions were two middle-aged women, the pair of them quite tipsy and clearly over-stimulated by their exotic surroundings. They'd never been to a lap dance club before, they informed me. One of them was enjoying herself so much that she shoved ten euro into the lap dancer's waistband. Before settling herself into the seat beside me. The dancer cast me a suspicious, reproachful glance, before disappearing into a dimly lit alcove with a staggering fat punter she was leading by the arm.

Larry Kennedy was in upbeat form. He lit a cigar and said to the women:

—Say hello to Auld Pappie! He's a terrific character so he is! A great man for the stories altogether. And certainly not the sort of fellow, I have to say, you'd expect to run into in a place like this! But then we all need our fun, even the hard-working family men! Isn't that right, Pappie? I'm telling you, ladies, a decenter man than this you'll never meet. Fucking mad about them kids of his, aren't you? You don't mind me saying that – do you, Auld Pappie?

I laughed and said:

—No, of course I don't, Larry, you know me better than that.

—Sure I do, friend. And all I can say is, you're a lucky man. That bitch of a wife of mine cleaned me out so she did, took everything. All because of a bit of a fling. Fuck her, that's what I say. One of the women rolled her eyes and giggled. The other lay back and kicked her heels in the air.

—Oh, you can laugh, girls. But it's no joke. Not when you're going through it. Shafted me proper over a one-night stand. I'm a bollocks for doing it that's what I am. But she's an even bigger one, to do the like of that to her husband. Now – who's for another drink?

The women ordered Bacardi-and-Cokes and tried their best to talk to me. But I had been drinking far too much and had become somewhat – no, excessively – morose and introspective. Despite my best efforts, I could not shake the gloominess off and presently the pair of them lost interest in me. I heard one of them whispering:

—He's too old. He wouldn't have any lead in his pencil, Jackie.

—You know there are rumours going around about him? My husband says he's not all that he seems.

I stiffened sharply the minute I heard her saying that. Because it had just dawned on me who her husband was – none other than the interfering driver. I felt my fist clenching but restrained myself admirably:

—Auld Pappie, I said, now be a good Pappie.

As I drove home from the club in the early hours of the morning, I cheered myself by thinking how absolutely perfect it had been for Ronan Collins to play a John Martyn record that day I'd found Catherine, when my search had come to an end. Or one which had sounded very much like him – husky and kind of deeply spiritual, otherworldly.

—May you never lay your head down without a hand to hold, I sang softly to myself.

It was a long way from the oppressive, furtive atmosphere of an obnoxious nightclub with its covetous, duplicitous, scrawny-legged dancers. And suspicious taxi drivers' wives muttering accusations against you. All inhabiting a place that held no attractions, a place that was dead and redundant, calcified.

For that was how it seemed to me now – a world of ash.

When compared with our crystal castle of the heart, our winterwood home where we'd endure for ever and beyond.

As Ned would say:

Till the very last pea was out of the pot,
Till the angels quit heaven's golden halls.

Fifteen: Let Me Rest
on Windy Mountain

WHEN I ANNOUNCED MY, admittedly, somewhat dramatic decision to leave Aungier Cabs and return home for good to Slievenageeha Mountain, everyone in the office was literally stunned.

Everyone, that is, apart from Larry Kennedy, who bawled out from the inside office:

—I knew it all along! Auld Pappie is a mountainer at heart! Oh yes, he might like to think he's a city-bred Dubliner like us but deep down, you'll find, he's a bona fide yokel! It's in their blood, you see. Sooner or later they all go back. But I'll tell you this, Pappie, we're all gonna miss you – ya great big hillbilly sheep-fucker you!

The rest of them were afraid that I might take offence. But they ought to have known me better than that. I was far too fond of Larry for that.

As well as that – the man had spoken the truth. For far too long I'd been living a lie.

The truth was that in my heart of hearts, I had never

liked the city. Had never, at any time, *truly* settled there. In spite of my persistent protests to the contrary. Particularly when I'd worked in RTE. To hear me then you'd have thought of me as just about as refined as they come: sounding off about wines and foreign travel. You'd have accepted me readily as a true-blue suburbanite, a Dubliner going back several generations. Until of course you got to know me, maybe thrown a bottle or two of wine inside me.

Perhaps then you might have experienced certain misgivings: revised, perhaps, your opinion entirely. After an hour or so listening to me incoherently blathering on about 'the ancient code of the hills' and what Slievenageeha had always privately meant to me. I might even have referred to a couple of 'enchanted days', fleetingly glimpsed through the thick mists of memory, which may not even have happened at all, back in the days when my mother had been alive. But which I continued to dwell on because I longed for them so much, right up to the moment – well, right up until the moment when I *expired*, in actual fact.

Which I did, I'm afraid at this juncture I have little choice but to reveal, late last year in the autumn of 2005, leaving instructions along with money that I be interred in Slievenageeha, the old home place, the Mountain of the Wind. Which may seem to some cynical, when you think of the things I've said about it in the past.

But there still is to be found there a peace and a sense of belonging, which I have succeeded in finding in no other place. A blissful peace and sense of place that no city on earth will ever be able to provide, certainly no city that I have ever visited, or am likely to now.

Now that I'm attired in my fine carved suit of boards, as Ned once remarked of a neighbour after a funeral.

Now that I've forsaken this world of pain.

I'd been lying there in the armchair for over two days when the police eventually broke down the door of the Sutton apartment where I'd continued living after Casey had moved out. There had already been references in the papers to 'important new developments' in the 'missing girl' case. With talk in some quarters of an arrest being imminent. Something which did not appear unlikely to me at all, certainly not after I arrived in one day to find the controller in grave conversation with a plain-clothes detective.

I remained out of sight, listening to what they were saying. By all accounts a decision had been taken to interview every cab driver in the base. I shivered when I heard Karen Venner's name, the American lady who had taken such exception to my behaviour that day at the Royal Dublin Hotel. I felt sick and stupid as I remembered my unnecessary gruffness. I became unsteady on my feet when I heard the detective use the words, quite matter-of-factly: 'internet appeal'.

I remembered the way Karen Venner had looked at me: as though, instinctively, she'd sensed something was indeed wrong, amiss.

As I stood there in the taxi office, clutching the door jamb, I was afraid at any moment I was going to faint. But just at that point, who went by, only the bold Larry Kennedy.

—Not a bad day, Larry! I chirped. If the rain keeps off we'll have no reason to complain!

—Now you're talking, Auld Pappie! he laughed.

The funeral ceremony took place, predictably enough, with no one at all present, just two days before 'A Winterwood Christmas'.

Which I'd been looking forward to for months, having bought their presents as far back as Halloween – a boxed set of John Martyn for Catherine, a cosmetic compact set for Immy, now that at last she'd become a young woman.

In keeping with the mood, a gale-force wind continued moaning throughout and the rain swept high above the rugged mountain peaks. It was lonesome, certainly, and there were better ways, no doubt, in which a man might have taken his leave. But at least I made it back – to Slievenageeha, my old mountain home.

If somewhat peremptorily cast, it has to be acknowledged, into a truly dark and dismal confinement which, it has been ordained, I must endure without protest. With my knees tucked tight against my chest, like some boy-sized crate of yellowed bones, shared with other equally lonely souls, in this barren ground where no roses grow.

The mountain proceeding, as it must, with the inevitable march of clamorous progress, as the Suzuki jeeps – which make their way to The Gold Club, their nocturnal roars like the triumphalist cheers of the living – are directed, without compassion, towards the cowed, defeated, and irrelevant dead.

*   *   *

Slievenageeha, proud Mountain of the Wind. The valley where I was born some sixty-four years ago, and once walked with my father by the babbling brook. Where we'd stand together as he stroked his red beard, placing his brawny, protective hand on my shoulder. As he said:

—There's one thing we can be sure of, Little Red. *Fanann na cnoic i bhfad uainn*. The hills will outlast us, Redmond, my son.

Before setting off together back to the old homestead, sitting there quietly in the silence of our humble mountain cabin. As he hummed a little and then lit up a stogie, reaching down for his jug of clear. In that old familiar mountain way.

A red beard. A weathered hand. A stogie.

Familiar details which really ought not to come as a surprise – not in a place where, like they say, every man is his own *grandmother*!

Or, as Casey liked to put it:

—Where every sonofabitch is an inbred twister!

With our red country heads and our 'auld' mountain ways. Of which my daddy was another prime example. Auld Daddy Hatch who had any amount of old mountain yarns. Who could effortlessly amuse at the drop of a hat. In that time-honoured, down-home, fireside way. You'd sit beside him as on he jabbered, knocking back mug after mug of the clear, with patches on his trousers and an old plaid shirt, sending a gobbet of spit into the fire as he battered on about the day they'd gone to town 'for the crack'. When their 'whole damned tribe' had got as 'drunk as monkeys'!

Fanciful yarns by the score he'd tell. Not to mention sing-songs and rip tunes from his fiddle. Hornpipes and polkas and jigs by the hundred. But then of course, that ought not to come as any surprise.

After all, wasn't he Florian's brother?

Florian Hatch, the well-known artiste?

Who loved to dance hornpipes in meadows behind trees?

And take photographs with the camera he had bought out in America?

And when he was finished whisper menacingly into your ear:

—Say a word about this and I'll murder you, Little Red. I'll murder you the way I done her.

The girl he claimed to have cut and cut badly, before eviscerating her and dumping her body. Somewhere out in America, it was claimed.

Of course he might not have done it at all.

But who was going to take the risk? Of deciding it was nothing but another example of a 'mountain tall tale'.

Certainly not an eight-year-old boy. Who just nibbled at his chocolate as the fiddle screeched wildly.

Trying not to squeal as its bow swept up and down.

The Present

Sixteen: The Strutting Living, the Creeping Dead

Slievenageeha Lidl IS THE name of the new retail centre in the town and Liebhraus is the construction company. The American microchip plant Intel employs in excess of 2,000 people with plans for further expansion already well advanced, towards what is predicted will be a mini Californian-style silicon valley. A spaghetti junction swirls way beyond the mountain. To accommodate the high-powered eighteen-wheeler diesel trucks, honking along the five-lane motorways, belching great clouds of thick smoky dust. The Gold Club really is jaw-droppingly spectacular. The five floors are designed in steel and glass and anything you want you can get it in there. Before five o' clock entry is free. It's like the gold rush days have come back to life, and it's in there you'll find your heart's desire, with no restrictions at all, just so long as you've got money and the right attitude about spending it. Once through its doors, you'll encounter flight attendants and kindergarten teachers, executives mingling with software engineers, all quaffing state-of-the-art cocktails, not batting an eyelid at the non-stop table dancing, or the inevitable quota of discreet working girls. You won't hear much country music either.

—No hillbillies here! you'll be told. No room for sheep-screwers in here, my friend!

The living strut and the dead souls creep.

I suppose that's the way it's meant to be. The way it's always been, right from the beginning, back in Old God's time.

—When the world was only a nipper and muggins wasn't even born, as Ned used to say.

Sometimes, whenever I feel like leaving it all behind, I'll creep, as I must, out of this dank hole and take myself for a walk across the valley, past the industrial park, down as far as the old babbling brook. The noise from Liebhraus can, at times, prove unbearable, the roar of diggers and drills and grinders like some mundane, prosaic but insanely dogged anti-symphony. So it's nice to sit here and listen to the waters babbling — right at the spot where, all those years ago, back in Old God's time, Ned Strange first walked out with Annamarie Gordon.

Annamarie Gordon who had promised to be his wife. Not only become his wife, in fact, but give him a son. She wanted it to happen, she told him. More than anything she wanted that to happen. So that they could be the Strange family together. And he could be their proud and doting father. Their 'Pappie'.

—It will be lovely, she said, 'Auld Pappie Strange', our son will call you. And you'll be a great father. I love you, Ned and always will. Do you know how much? I'll love you till the seas run dry. Till the seas run dry and the angels quit heaven. That's how much, my love, and more.

It was in honour of the memory of that never-to-be-born boy that one day after sitting by the brook I set myself the task of fashioning a little commemorative cross. I'd watched my mother making them out of rushes, in the long ago when I too was very small. Before she had died like an angel in the chapel.

But I couldn't bear to think about that any more. All I wanted to do was lay my cross on the cemetery grass, in honour of the sweet little 'neverborn'. To kneel on that grass and whisper a silent prayer. So I made my memorial and set off on my mission.

It had already begun to snow as I drifted across the valley. It swept in flurries as I placed the cross on the cold stony ground. Marking the spot where *nothing* would ever be.

Because, of course, Ned Strange never did have a son. No, no 'baby Owen' was ever to be delivered of Annamarie Gordon, for Ned Strange or anyone else.

Or of Catherine Courtney for Redmond Hatch either. No babies for couples whose love had turned to dust.

Which was why I had hand-lettered across the cross's centre:

Little Rose of the Outlands: we'd have loved you so much
RIP 00 AD–00 AD

—The most wanted of all that never was to be: a love that died before it truly lived. Baby Owen. Redmond Hatch and Catherine Courtney.

I whisper those words to myself in the nights. As I lie here listening to his tense, covetous breathing. The breathing of who?

Why, His Eminence Ned Strange: the Son of Perdition, King of the Air. Who now – and for ever, apparently – is to be my nearest neighbour. Something which ought not to come as a surprise to anyone. Not in a community celebrated for being close-knit. Not in a place that's been called 'Incest Mountain'.

Which, as it turns out, is most apt indeed. With Ned and I being so close now that he's aware of practically every one of my thoughts. Generally before I am myself. After all, he's a very powerful man. Why he can even, you know, predict the future.

—What exactly did you expect? he says to me. You can't say I didn't warn you. Something dreadful's what I promised, something dreadful's what you got. It's nothing more than you ought to have expected.

Eternity

Seventeen: Little Red,
the Outland Rose

IT WAS THE 22ND of February 2004 and there could be no doubt about it — Redmond Hatch was just about the happiest man alive. He was positively glowing with happiness as he boarded the tube train that would take him to Kilburn, an inner suburb of North London. And proceeded to walk the streets where once upon a time he had resided for three wonderfully happy and fruitful years. Whistling absent-mindedly as he strolled along the main thoroughfare of Kilburn High Road and sat on a wooden bench in Queen's Park to feed the pigeons. Just as he'd once done with his beloved daughter Imogen.

—Tell me about winterwood, he heard her say, tell me about it again, Daddy. And Redmond Hatch described it in detail. Right down to the Princess of Winter in her white satin gown. And the robins who guarded its snow-speckled portals.

—Did you ever see a robin cry? his daughter had asked him.

—No, he replied, because in winterwood they're happy.

But no sooner had he said it than Redmond Hatch found himself shivering, for an idiotic reason – he'd imagined a bearded tramp going by had looked like, why, like Ned Strange, of all people. It had momentarily troubled him that he should think such a thing. At this point, now – after all this time. But he succeeded in persuading himself that the idea was nothing short of idiotic. Belonging to a distant, long-forgotten time. A time of irrational stress and tension. When he'd been locked in a struggle with someone, above all, who didn't even exist. He looked again and, predictably of course, the tramp was gone, nowhere to be seen. Redmond shook his head, reflecting quite good-humouredly on the absurdity of it all.

It had been a long journey, he told himself, as he made his way back to Kilburn station, the rattling tube speeding onwards across North London. And, at times, a difficult one. But, in spite of everything, it had been worth it. A face distorted in the window opposite suddenly caught his eye. Almost aggressively, he lifted his head and stared directly at it, apprehending it for nothing more or less than what it was: the weary and weather-beaten countenance of an elderly female vagrant, grinding her gums beneath a plastic hood. He released a soft and contented private laugh, thinking to himself how such a fleeting and commonplace banality would once upon a time have been invested with significance, resulting in unsettling and perhaps even dangerous consequences. He rested his palms on his thighs and stared at the old lady, once more experiencing the most luxurious, even delirious calm, just as the train began to slow, making its approach towards Bond Street.

For it was a time of great personal triumph for Redmond Hatch, of positively enviable achievement and success. A trend now set to continue that very night, as his documentary film *These Are My Mountains* had been nominated in four different categories of the Celtic Film and Television Awards which were to be presented that evening at a grand gala function in the Grosvenor House Hotel. He would have been overjoyed if Casey could have accompanied him. But she'd been acting a little strangely of late. Pressure of work, she'd explained when he asked her.

—*These Are My Mountains*, he heard the judges declare, is an anatomy of a society in flux, a magnificently detailed view of the journey from the almost medieval atmosphere of 1930s rural Ireland to the buoyant postmodern European country it is today, and must be considered a uniquely seminal and passionate work.

Redmond was deeply moved by this praise, and also by the analysis of the adjudicators, which he found simultaneously informative and perceptive. Consequently he was somewhat taken aback when, on his return from the men's room, he found himself gripped by a panic attack of such severity that it blurred his vision and weakened his limbs to such an extent that he had no choice but to return to the toilet stall. Sitting there, as cold perspiration broke out on his skin, he heard an unmistakable voice:

—Redmond, it's me, Edmund. I'm waiting for you, Redmond. Soon we'll be together. In the hills.

He fervently prayed the attack would pass. But then, even more tantalisingly, to his ears came drifting the softest of whispers:

—What can I do, my love fond and true, but shield you from wind and weather?

His teeth were clenched and his heart was pounding. His shirt, he realised, was soaking too. He tried to get up but remained in the cubicle for some considerable time, his head clutched in his hands. He began to fear that these feelings might not only fail to pass after a reasonable passage of time, but conceivably, in fact, might *never* do so! Thankfully, however, this did not prove to be the case – the attack, eventually, began to recede and gradually his courage began to reassert itself.

And when, once more, he appeared in the magnificent banqueting hall, no one would ever have suspected that anything at all untoward had occurred. He helped himself to a glass of champagne and, as he sipped it, quite on the spur of the moment, decided to place a telephone call home, to Casey. To his surprise, he received no reply. With repeated attempts proving equally unsatisfactory. What of it, he explained to himself, she's probably just fallen asleep. He swanned back into the centre of the hall and committed himself to enjoying to the full what remained of a very special evening.

—I can call her later from the hotel, he said to himself.

Nonetheless, the source of his agitation subtly refused to go away, and he found himself once more becoming irascible, finding fault, first with the drinks and then with the food, to the bored dismay of passing waiters. No matter how he tried, he could not, for the life of him, understand why she might be asleep. He checked his watch again. It wasn't late – just after eleven. Casey rarely retired before twelve. He looked up to see one of the judges hastening towards him.

—This is Sinclair Evans, he was told, he absolutely adores your work. A fellow Celt, of course, Mr Tiernan.

It was a wonderful stroke of luck, meeting someone like Sinclair Evans: one of the most singular and knowledgable men Redmond had encountered. His knowledge, not just of cinema, but of the world of art in general, was most impressive. Redmond could have listened to him all night. And did. They were both quite tipsy when the evening, at last, began drawing to a close. But it had been terrific. An absolutely wonderful night, thought Redmond to himself. He could barely even remember the 'anxiety attack', or however you might choose to describe the irritating inconvenience, which was all it really amounted to now.

With the result that, in spite of the driving rain, he simply couldn't have been more contented as he stood with his award in a plastic bag outside the Metropole Hotel in Edgware Road, generously tipping the African cab driver. He paused for a moment to pocket his change. A clap of thunder rumbled sullenly in the distance, followed by the sound of sharp clipped footsteps. The hooded youth who suddenly appeared hesitated momentarily before breaking into a run.

—Can't you get out of the way? Redmond heard him cry,

stumbling awkwardly, the coins rolling from his hand. He
bawled after him:

—What's your problem? I said, what's your fucking
problem!

He was taken aback when the youth stopped, staring
menacingly back at him. Then, out of nowhere, another
youth appeared.

—He giving you trouble? he called out to his mate. This
fucking cunt, he giving you trouble?

The youth turned and spat at him, swearing loudly
before taking off. A truck roared by, soaking Redmond's
suit as he haplessly gathered up his change.

He made his way through the revolving door. The night
porter gave him a reassuring smile.

—Bad night, he said. Much thunder.

—Much thunder, agreed Redmond, still clutching the
handful of wet coins in his fist. More likely than not he'd
exaggerated the potential threat, he told himself, sighing
contentedly as he crossed the lobby floor. Probably the
nerves of the prize-giving and everything, and that unfortunate business in the toilet stall. In any case, he realised,
it made no difference for any minute he'd be talking to
Casey and that was all he cared about now. He saw himself
sitting on the bed as he said:

—They really loved it. They loved the film, Casey.

He pressed the elevator button. On the third floor he was
joined by another late-night reveller, a fellow countryman
as it turned out.

—What is it you have in the bag? Batman, the Irishman

laughed, staggering slightly as he stared at Redmond's award pushing its way out of its plastic confinement. It was a bronze figure with spreading wings.

—*The Death of Nuada*, brave warrior of the Celts, he told him, it was specially cast.

—Oh! said the Irishman, a little disappointed, I thought 'twas fucking Batman! The Irishman belched and said:

—Too much Kronenbourg again, I'm afraid!

Redmond smiled and nodded sympathetically.

—I've had quite a few myself tonight! he laughed.

The thunder was still audible, but fainter now. The Irishman looked at him stupidly and staggered on one foot, raising his thumb for no apparent reason. In spite of himself, Redmond couldn't stop thinking about the incident outside. Stupid as it was, his thoughts kept on returning to it.

—He giving you trouble? This fucking cunt, he giving you trouble?

He stepped through the parting elevator doors. The Irishman was calling something after him but he couldn't hear him. He pushed his key card into the slot. As soon as he got in, he tore off his drenched suit bottoms and made straight for the telephone. He lifted the receiver and dialled the number. It was just at that moment he heard the faint murmurs of a fragile, plaintive, almost heart-breaking voice. It sounded too sweet to have been alarming. But it was. In fact it was so alarming that there aren't any words which might, with any degree of accuracy at least, even begin to describe it.

—Please help me, Daddy. It's me, Pinkie Pie.

For the briefest of moments he was tempted to laugh.

Attributing this absurd turn of events, yet again, to his infuriatingly overactive imagination, the product of another unfortunate and extremely stressful night. He relaxed somewhat as the silence began to return. Then, even softer than before, he heard his daughter – for it was unmistakably her – plead once more:

—Daddy? Please, Daddy. Can you hear me?

He shot upright and stood there, primed. The voice was coming from the direction of the bathroom.

—Daddy, will you come to me? I need you, Daddy. Please come to me.

His heart was beating furiously as he approached the bathroom door. Standing there in his boxer shorts, the worst fear he had ever experienced numbed his entire body.

—It's cold out here in winterwood, Daddy.

—Jesus! he cried aloud.

—Daddy, is that you? Daddy, will you come in?

He stood in the bathroom doorway, chafing helplessly at his knuckles. He could see her clearly behind the shower curtain, her little helpless, shivering silhouette reaching out to him.

—Imogen darling! Immy, it's OK!

He flung himself forward and tore frantically at the plastic curtain, the brass rings skittering dissonantly as he found himself embracing – not his daughter, but a cold stiff figure covered in excrement, its neck looped in a cord, its curling lip frozen in a rictus of cruel malignity.

—Like I said, whispered Ned, when it happened, Redmond, you'd *know*.

*   *   *

Nothing would give me greater pleasure than to allow Redmond Hatch to conclude his own story. Regrettably, however, that is impossible. There are times, it has to be acknowledged, when he will make the most valiant efforts. But somehow he never seems to transcend a certain point. When he finds himself in a certain hotel bathroom, standing mutely beside a torn shower curtain.

After that, I'm afraid, he appears to lose the power of speech, just sits there staring, uttering sounds which are quite indecipherable. Certainly making no sense. Poor fellow. It really is dreadful. It must have been quite an ordeal.

Which is why it must inevitably come to me to finish his story, me, his oldest friend and neighbour on the mountain. A task for which I hope I am adequately equipped. Which I ought to be, of course. Although, given my reputation, one runs the risk of certain liberties being taken with what, after all, is a straightforward narrative. Of my inserting certain 'flourishes' of a certain 'fanciful' nature perhaps. As us old mountain fiddlers have been known to do.

But not this time. For, after all, there is hardly any need. There being quite enough drama, one might suggest, in his private little 'melodrama' already.

After arriving back earlier than had been expected from London, Redmond Hatch spent some hours waiting across the street from his home in the north Dublin suburb of Sutton. Presently the front door opened and he saw James Ingram the broadcaster emerge. He was pulling on his jacket and laughing. He chatted with Casey for a moment before kissing her, then swung off, turning one last time to bid her goodbye.

—Love you, he called.

—Love you, Casey replied, blowing him a kiss. She was wearing her dressing gown over her negligee. There were little blue ribbons all down its front. Redmond knew because he had bought it for her. Had purchased it – quite coincidentally – in Harrods of London, the very same place where Catherine and he had got the coat for Immy. He watched Casey now as she pulled the dressing gown around her.

—Love you, called James Ingram, leaning out of the car window. I'll ring you later, yeah? Ciao!

Before rolling up the window and driving off, happily, like any man would. Any man lucky enough to be in love.

Redmond's subsequent departure from RTE proved rather sudden indeed, with something quite spectacularly incoherent mumbled to a perplexed Head of Programmes regarding a certain 'job offer with the BBC'.

A tall tale indeed, a fanciful yarn and make no mistake. In its lack of verisimilitude and sheer implausibility rivalled only perhaps by the suggestion of a grown man driving his car nightly to a copse of pine on the outskirts of the city to read at length from both Raymond Briggs's *The Snowman* and the Scandinavian Maurice Sendak's *Where the Wild Things Are* for the benefit of his adored darling wife and child.

And in no way comparable to the rather underwhelming nature of his own actual demise, surrounded by the policemen who'd taken a hatchet to his door, with a bottle of the clear lying empty in his lap and on the floor beside him, the *Sunday Independent*, with its headline 'THE INNOCENTS: A NATION MOURNS', just above a photo of Catherine Courtney and her daughter.

The rest being history, as the storytellers are fond of saying.

With the remains of Redmond Hatch being ferried back to Slievenageeha Cemetery, his dying wishes laudably being respected, before, with the minimum of ceremony, being conveniently delivered — into whose uncommonly patient and tender loving arms, do you suppose?

Why mine, of course, the extended extremities of Auld Ned Strange, to whom they had been promised a long time ago, and who in turn had promised to shield his charge from the vagaries of wind and weather. Outside a church one otherwise entirely unremarkable day, on Harold's Cross Road, to the south of Dublin city.

Redmond's eyes, when they opened, registered the most pleasant surprise — as he realised, to his delight, that he was not being confronted by some unspeakable, unimaginable horror as might reasonably have been expected, but by a frosted light refracting through the intersecting branches of the trees and a radiant vision of the woman he had loved, attired in the most beautiful long dress of the whitest satin, with a glittering silver tiara on her head, parting her lace veil as she emerged from the pines. Approaching him, she softly murmured: 'May you never lay your head down without a hand to hold', then lowered herself on to him ever so gently, whispering sweetly into his ear. Calling him 'darling' as she stroked his hair, before touching his neck with her tender 'sugar lips'.

At which point the blood began to comprehensively drain from his face, as he emitted his first sad, pitiable whimper.

Realising just who his companion was, as I flashed my incisors and drew him towards me: Little Red.

Slipping the chocolate bar into his hand, as we lay there together beneath the tall pines, before looking up to see them falling: the very first flakes of the most beautiful winter snow.

A NOTE ON THE AUTHOR

Patrick McCabe was born in Ireland in 1955. His novels include *Music on Clinton Street, Carn, The Butcher Boy* and *Breakfast on Pluto*, both of which were shortlisted for the Booker Prize. *The Butcher Boy* won the Irish Times/Aer Lingus Literature Prize in 1992 and was made into a film, directed by Neil Jordan, in 1997. The film *Breakfast on Pluto*, also directed by and co-written with Neil Jordan, was released in 2006, to great acclaim. Patrick McCabe lives in his home town of Clones, County Monaghan.

A NOTE ON THE TYPE

Linotype Garamond Three – based on seventeenth century copies of Claude Garamond's types, cut by Jean Jannon. This version was designed for American Type Founders in 1917, by Morris Fuller Benton and Thomas Maitland Cleland and adapted for mechanical composition by Linotype in 1936.